SISTER WIFE

SHELLEY HRDLITSCHKA

ORCA BOOK PUBLISHERS

Library and Archives Canada Cataloguing in Publication

Hrdlitschka, Shelley, 1956-
Sister wife / written by Shelley Hrdlitschka.

ISBN 978-1-55143-927-3

I. Title.

PS8565.R44S58 2008   jC813'.54   C2008-903022-2

First published in the United States, 2008
Library of Congress Control Number: 2008928548

Summary: In a remote polygamist community, Celeste struggles to accept her
destiny while longing to be free to live her life her way.

Orca Book Publishers gratefully acknowledges the support for its publishing
programs provided by the following agencies: the Government of Canada through
the Book Publishing Industry Development Program and the Canada Council for the
Arts, and the Province of British Columbia through the BC Arts Council
and the Book Publishing Tax Credit.

Design by Teresa Bubela
Cover photography by Masterfile

ORCA BOOK PUBLISHERS
PO Box 5626, STN. B
VICTORIA, BC CANADA
V8R 6S4

ORCA BOOK PUBLISHERS
PO Box 468
CUSTER, WA USA
98240-0468

www.orcabook.com
Printed and bound in Canada.
Printed on 100% PCW recycled paper.

12 11 10 09 • 5 4 3 2

SISTER WIFE

For Sue, my true-blue friend, with love and appreciation.

ACKNOWLEDGMENTS

Heartfelt thanks once again to Beryl Young, Kim Denman and Diane Tullson for being so much more than just a writing critique group.

The inuksuk is a symbol with deep roots in the Inuit culture. It's a directional marker that signifies safety, hope and friendship. It speaks to a spirit, to what's inside us, yet its meaning is whatever the builder gives it.

Chapter One

CELESTE

I am consumed with impure thoughts. My head is swirling with stories that would give the Prophet heart failure if he knew of them. I fear that I am destined for eternal damnation.

I haven't always been like this. The stories started when Taviana came to Unity. She wasn't born and raised here like the rest of us but was found on the outside, living on the streets, doing unspeakable things. Jacob, an elder, wanted to help her, so he brought her to us, and she was so grateful that she's worked hard to learn the rules of our faith. Now she understands and appreciates that obedience is the only path to Heaven, but sometimes she slips up, and when we're working side by side, she tells me stories she heard as a little girl.

I know that the only stories I need to hear are ones that will keep my mind pure, and those ones are all contained in the sacred book, so I shouldn't listen to Taviana.

But the way she tells them! She puts on voices, and sometimes she even acts them out. I have to listen, and before you know it I hear myself begging for another one. Right now I'm filled with remorse just thinking about my part in this activity, but I can't seem to help myself.

Today I'm reminded of the story she told a few weeks ago, the one of the boy named the Pied Piper. He was some sort of gypsy who wandered into town playing a flute. The music appeared to cast a spell on the children, and they followed him everywhere. When she told the story, I imagined that the Pied Piper looked just like Jon, tall and slim, with wind-tousled hair. He'd have soft brown eyes that looked right into your soul, and he wasn't a show-off like the other boys.

I DON'T HAVE a flute, but I have a flock of small children following me from the school to the playground near the river, where I help mind them until it's time to start with the supper chores. I'm trying to remember what eventually became of the Pied Piper and those children. I'll have to ask Taviana the next time we're alone.

I purposely lead the group on the route that passes the Nielsson farm, hoping to get a glimpse of Jon. I'm not disappointed. He's outside, working with a group of other boys. It looks like they're repairing a fence, but there's a lot of goofing off going on. When Jon sees us trudging along, he looks at me—right in the eyes! Then he smiles, a shy smile. I find myself smiling back but quickly look away. My heart patters in my chest and my cheeks burn.

I try pushing the thoughts out of my head, but it's impossible. My brain just gets filled with them. I'm supposed to remain pure of mind and body for my future husband. My thoughts of Jon are not at all pure, and it scares me that I can't stop them. I find myself making up stories about him, and I add to them whenever I get a chance. There's the Jon-and-I-alone-at-the-river story, wading into the freezing water, shrieking with delight as our feet go numb. Then there's the Jon-and-I-lying-in-the-meadow story. We're staring up at the clouds together, his hand holding mine. My mind has been taken over by an evil imagination monster, and I'm helpless to make it go away. To be honest, I don't know that I even want it to. I want eternal life, of course, but thinking of Jon makes the time pass when the chores seem endless. At least I'm still pure of body.

With these thoughts of my salvation, or lack of it, weighing me down, I struggle to play with the children, skipping stones in the water, making daisy chains and handing out bread and cheese from the snack basket.

"C'mon, Celeste," Rebecca whines, tugging on my skirt. "Let's play hide-and-go-seek."

Rebecca is my four-year-old sister who I'm particularly fond of, but I can't even find the patience for her today. "Rebecca, can't you see I'm busy?" I snap, and I push her hand away. The hurt look on her little face irritates me. I continue packing up the picnic basket.

Nanette appears beside me. "Go, Celeste," she whispers, motioning toward the river. "Take a walk or read from the book. It's okay."

Nanette, my next youngest sister, has been watching me. She knows that child minding is my least favorite chore, and I know she won't report me for taking a break. She's like the Pied Piper herself: she loves playing with the children. I'll give her a break from one of our other chores later. And she's right. I do need to get away from these children today. I grab my sack and set off toward the bend in the river where I can relax, unobserved. Propping myself against a tree, I close my eyes and soak up the warm afternoon sun. I try to keep my thoughts pure, I really do, but once again I find myself returning to my latest story, the one where Jon and I are living in a faraway cabin, just the two of us, no little children, no sister wives...

When I finally open my eyes again, I notice a figure farther down the river. It's a boy, or maybe a young man, and I know he's not from Unity because he's wearing shorts and nothing else. He appears to be piling large rocks, one on top of the other. He keeps wandering away from his project but then returning to it, bent over with the weight of a new rock. Eventually he sits on the beach to admire his creation. After a couple of minutes, he gets up, stretches, adjusts a couple of the rocks and then wanders off downstream before disappearing around a corner.

Hiking my dress up over my ankles, I cross the stony beach to take a look at the rock formation. As I get closer, I can see that the rocks have been stacked to look like a little human. There are two blocky legs, a couple of large flat stones representing a body, and another two stones that reach out as arms. This is topped off with a rectangular stone—the neck—and then a somewhat smaller round stone—the head.

I wonder at the meaning of this little statue. I've heard the Prophet speak of the danger of pagan symbols. Is this something evil that I should destroy?

I circle him a couple of times. He's a squat little fellow who looks happy, despite his lack of facial features. He can't possibly be evil. I find myself smiling at him, and I'm reluctant to leave him there all alone on the beach. How can I just walk away? I have an idea.

Struggling because of my long skirt, I begin to create my own rock formation beside him. First the legs. The rocks must be evenly sized and ones that can lie securely on top of one another. This isn't too hard. I have to search farther down the beach to find large stones that work as a body. If they're too heavy, I can't carry them across the beach, but they have to be substantial enough to represent the trunk. I find I can't hike up my skirt and haul rocks at the same time, so I tuck the hem of my skirt into the waistband of my apron.

Finding long flat stones that can rest on the body as arms is my next challenge. I try to balance them on the torso but they simply drop off the sides. I place a heavier rock on top of the body and then slide the arms under it. That works, and now my statue also has a neck. I carefully balance a head on top.

My statue looks nothing like the first figure, but just like it too. They stand side by side, sturdy, guarding the river that rushes past. They are just rocks, yet they have such character. And they have a connection. I have created one of them. Have I ever created anything before? And how can something I made from plain old river rock bring me so much satisfaction? I don't know, but it does.

I sit back to ponder my handiwork. And then I hear my sister calling me. "Celeste! Let's go!"

I've completely forgotten the time. With a last glance at the statues, I gather up my dress and scramble across the beach to rejoin Nanette and her band of merry children, which is what I've secretly been calling them ever since Taviana told me the story of Robin Hood.

"C'MON, CELESTE," Nanette whispers, poking me in the shoulder. "There must be at least one man you can picture yourself married to."

I roll over to face her and pull the blankets back up to our necks. One of our little sisters, curled up in a crowded bed beside ours, sighs in her sleep.

"I keep telling you, Nanette," I whisper back. "There just isn't." I don't mention anything about Jon. I *can* imagine being married to him, but he's not technically a man, and she only asked about men. Even though Nanette enjoys fantasizing about marriage, I know that she would be shocked if she knew where my mind has been taking me lately. It goes without saying that making up stories about being alone with a boy is wrong. Girls in our faith are assigned to men, not boys. Nanette is pure. She has internalized the rules. She finds joy in being obedient. Was I ever like that?

"How about Harold?" she suggests.

"Are you kidding! He's cross-eyed and an old grouch. Yuck."

"Okay, then how about Graham?"

I think about Graham. At least he isn't *that* old yet. "No way. His first wife, Elizabeth, she's always cranky. I could never share a home with her."

"Todd?"

"Way too fat. And creepy."

"But, Celeste, just think how much fun it will be to look after your own babies instead of someone else's."

My eyes are adjusting to the dark, and I can now make out the freckles that cover thirteen-year-old Nanette's nose and forehead. She's a year younger than I am, but already she's pining to be married and raise a family, just like a good girl should. I understand wanting to get out of this house, but wanting to have babies?

"You're right about that," I tell her. "I am tired of looking after other people's babies."

"See? It's going to be wonderful! I just wish I knew who I was going to be assigned to."

"The time will come soon enough, Nanette."

"Not soon enough for me," she sighs, closing her eyes. "But very soon for you."

I don't answer but pull her closer and we snuggle together, waiting for sleep to come.

Nanette and I have shared a bed for as long as I can remember. I cannot imagine sharing one with anyone else. I've listened to my mother's sister wives whispering in the kitchen, giggling, so I have an idea about what sleeping with a husband means, what you have to do with them to have babies. With Jon I can imagine it, I even yearn for it. With a husband who may be older than Daddy…yuck! A shudder runs through me.

"What's wrong, Celeste?" Nanette's eyes have popped open again.

"Nothing. Go to sleep."

She studies me for a moment and then closes her eyes.

Having lots of babies is required, but at least I won't have to sleep with him every night. Some nights I'll be alone. Whoever my husband is, he'll have to take turns sleeping with each of his wives. That's the one good thing about having sister wives.

In less than a minute, I can feel Nanette's breathing change as she drifts into sleep. I twist a lock of her soft hair between my fingers and feel her warm breath on my cheek. Have I ever shared her unquestioning faith? Maybe I did, a long time ago, though Daddy has always said that I ask too many questions for my own good. He tells me I should be more like Nanette, that I should practice purity and keep sweet.

If only I could.

❧ Chapter Two ❧

Taviana

"The dishwasher was the only good thing about home," I tell Celeste, placing another dry plate on the towering stack. She's washing the dishes so fast I can barely keep up. With thirty-two of us living here, washing dishes is one big chore.

"I still don't understand how a machine can wash dishes, Taviana," Celeste says.

"It's simple," I tell her. "There are racks that hold 'em. You put the dirty ones in, add soap, turn it on and presto! Water swishes around and cleans everything. About an hour later you just have to put them all away."

"Kind of like putting the dishes in a sink with soapy water, swishing them around and then putting them in the drying rack. I don't see that it would make much difference. You still have to put them away."

I think about that. "Your hands don't get wet with a dishwasher, and no one has to dry."

Celeste shrugs and then glances about to see who might be listening. "I just think it would be better if there were fewer kids," she whispers.

"You want me to leave?" I ask, putting on my most offended face.

She flicks soapy water at me. "Not you, silly!" She lowers her voice. "You and Nanette are what make this place bearable. It's all the little ones. They're too small to help, but they make such a mess and they need so much attention. I never get my mother or Daddy to myself."

I glance at Celeste's face as I run the dishtowel over another plate. She's grouchy, as usual. I prefer doing chores with Nanette, who's always cheerful. She's also drop-dead gorgeous. Maybe it's a good thing she's in this old-fashioned place because in the real world a girl who looks like Nanette would attract way too much attention. She's only thirteen, but under her long dress she looks more like eighteen, and she has the kind of chiseled face you'd expect to see on the front of a fashion magazine.

But I'll never forget how welcome Celeste made me feel when I first arrived. Most of the women and girls gave me looks, and I knew they didn't think Jacob should have brought me here. Celeste seemed stoked to meet someone from outside The Movement, and she's always firing questions at me. I try to return the favor by telling her stories, even though I know I'm not supposed to. She's just so curious, and the stories make her smile.

"So what eventually happened to the Pied Piper?" she asks, quietly, while pulling the plug from the bottom of the sink.

I have to wrack my brain to remember. "I think he led all the kids out of town, never to return again."

She looks horrified. "He wasn't a good person?"

I shrug and add one last plate to the stack. "He was just angry. He'd been hired to lure all the rats and mice out of town, which he did. But then the mayor didn't pay him, so he got even by luring all the children away."

"That's awful!"

"It's just a story, Celeste."

"But why couldn't it have a happy ending?"

"That would be boring," I tell her and snap the tea towel at her backside, but even with that I can't get a smile out of her today.

I find Nanette at the back of the sprawling house, ironing. She grins when she sees me. I make myself useful by folding towels that are heaped in another basket. "How come Celeste is always so grouchy?" I ask her.

"That's just the way she is," Nanette says. "Daddy says she thinks too much."

I pull another towel out of the basket and consider that. There is such a routine here, such a structured lifestyle, that I suppose a person doesn't really need to think much at all. Conformity is what they strive for, not individuality. Everything is laid out, from what you're expected to contribute right down to what you wear. Even your husband or wife is chosen for you. Maybe it's not the thinking that is Celeste's problem, but the questioning.

"When you're finished here," I say, "do you want to go for a walk?"

"Sure," Nanette says. "I'll just check with Mother first, to see what else has to be done."

Nanette had to rock one of the twins to sleep, and I had to make sandwiches for the following day, but finally we're on the dirt road that winds its way through town. The sun has just set and the mountain range to the east appears black against the indigo sky. Nanette reaches out and takes my hand. I squeeze hers back and we stroll along in a peaceful silence. Nanette is the sister I always dreamed of having.

Just as we're rounding the last bend before the road would take us right out of town, we pass the Nielsson farm. I can hear hushed voices and I smell cigarette smoke, which is unheard of in Unity. Peering into the twilight, I see that there's a group of guys gathered outside the barn. They're straddling farm equipment and sitting on the flatbed of a pickup truck. Their heads turn in unison as they notice us. Nanette squeezes my hand a little tighter.

"Want to turn around?" I ask her quietly.

She glances at the guys and nods. As we turn back, one of them calls out, "Good evening, ladies. Care to join us?"

"Don't say anything," Nanette instructs quietly.

I look down at her and am surprised to see how frightened she looks. Then I glance back at the boys. They look harmless enough, even though I see a flask being passed between two of them, guys who I don't recognize.

"Why don't we just go over and say hi?" I suggest, my curiosity getting the best of me.

"No," she whispers firmly. "Three of those boys are apostates. Don't go near them."

Now I get it. An apostate is someone who has been kicked out of the community. They're considered "tools of the devil," and Nanette probably figures they're here to poison the minds of our pure boys. Maybe they are, but what she doesn't understand is that the life I lived before coming here is probably way more sinful than what any of these boys can even imagine. I don't miss that life, but sometimes I long to hang out with guys my own age. My opportunity has arrived. I drop Nanette's hand. "You go on home," I tell her. "I'll be there in a few minutes."

"You're not going to talk to them!" she says, horrified.

"Just for a bit," I tell her. "Don't worry, Nanette," I add, tugging her long braid. "I know how to handle guys. I was an old pro at it before I came here."

Not a good choice of words, I realize. She regards me seriously and glances back at the boys. "I don't like this," she says quietly. She gives me a disapproving look, turns and walks away.

I watch her disappear into the darkening night. Then I find myself hiking up my skirt and scrambling over a fence. "How's it going?" I ask, walking up to the group.

It takes a moment for any of them to answer. I suppose they are as stunned as Nanette that I actually joined them. Then the boy with the lit cigarette speaks. "You must be Taviana," he says.

"I am. How did you know?"

"Because no girl who was raised in Unity would've climbed that fence the way you just did." He's regarding me with admiration.

I shrug. "Okay, but how do you know my name?"

"I live in Highrock now. The people on the streets there are still talking about you. You're like an urban legend or something."

Highrock is where I used to live, before Jacob rescued me. I quickly change the subject. "So what's your name?"

"Lucas."

"And what brings you here, Lucas?"

He takes a long drag on a cigarette. "I'm just back for a visit, to say hi."

I nod and glance around at the faces of the other boys. The ones from Unity are looking slightly embarrassed by my presence, but one of the other strangers pulls the flask out of his back pocket and takes a swig.

"Is it true what they say about you, Taviana?" he asks while sliding the bottle back into his pocket.

I look directly at him. He looks away. "Probably," I tell him. "What's it to you?"

"Just wondering if you still…"

"No," I tell him. "That's why I moved here." I look at the other boys. "So, who are the rest of you?"

A third stranger, who looks a little older than the rest, offers his name first. "I'm Jimmy," he says. He bows slightly and adds, "Pleased to meet you, Taviana."

I bow slightly back. "And I'm pleased to meet you, Jimmy."

A Unity boy, who couldn't be more than twelve years old, speaks up. "I'm Stephen Nielsson."

"Hi, Stephen," I say, smiling at him. He blushes deeply.

"I'm Cameron," a slightly older boy says. "Stephen's cousin."

I nod at Cameron. He's very cute, in an innocent way. I think of Nanette and wonder how girls here can remain so self-disciplined when it comes to these boys. I turn to the last boy. "And you're…?"

"Jon," he says and smiles.

There's something so sweet, so refreshing, about Jon's face that I can hardly drag my eyes away. My physical response to him is something I haven't felt in a couple of years, something I thought I might never feel again. It takes me by surprise.

"So what are you guys doing?" I ask, looking around and hoping I've masked my reaction to Jon's smile.

"Just hanging," flask-boy says, and I realize I never asked him his name. I also note that he didn't offer it.

I turn back to Lucas. "How come you left Unity?" I ask him.

He studies my face for a while, and I sense he's trying to figure out how to answer that question. "I had a…a clash of values with the Prophet, you might say. I wanted more in my life than I could ever get here."

"More in your life?" I ask. "Like cigarettes and booze?" I gesture toward his friend.

He studies me a little longer and then shakes his head, as if dismissing me. "Have you found in Unity what you came looking for?" he asks.

"I didn't actually come here looking for anything. I was invited here. And I like what I've found. It's safe."

Lucas grunts. "Yeah, well, you won't be here long if you keep jumping fences to talk to guys. Don't you know they don't like that kind of thing?"

I just shrug, but his words sting. I nod. "You're right, Lucas. I just wanted to be friendly, but I guess I should go." I turn to look for the gate and pull up my dress slightly to make walking easier. "See you guys around," I call over my shoulder.

It has gotten much darker, and I hope I'm walking toward where the gate is. When I get there, I realize that what I thought was a gate, isn't. I begin following the fence that runs parallel to the road. If I have to climb over it again, I want to do it where the boys can't see me.

Suddenly I hear running footsteps approaching me from behind. I whirl around, expecting to find flask-boy following me, looking for a little action, but I come face to face with the guy called Jon.

"Hey," I say, startled.

"Hi," he says. "Are you looking for the gate?"

"Yeah, which way is it?"

He points in the direction I'm walking. "Just a little farther."

"Thanks." I smile at him and force myself to keep walking. I'm worried that if I talk to him any longer, I might slide back into some old habits, like flirting. That would probably scare this innocent boy off. Yet this guy has clearly rekindled feelings I've tucked away.

"Can I walk with you, show you where it is?" he asks.

I hesitate before I answer, and in that moment I see a look of concern cross his face. "I mean you no harm!" he says.

"I know you don't," I answer, and I smile at him. "Yeah, c'mon, Jon. Show me to the gate."

We walk along in silence for a moment, and then I ask, "So why are those guys in Unity tonight?"

It takes him a moment to answer. "They just like to come around and tell us what it's like to live in different places."

"How would your parents feel if they knew you were talking with them?"

"They wouldn't like it much." He hesitates. "So I hope you don't mention it to anyone."

"Your secret is safe with me, Jon."

I think about my earlier conversation with Celeste, the one about the Pied Piper. Maybe these guys visiting from the outside are a modern-day version of the same guy, only this time he's only interested in the boy children.

"Here's the gate," Jon says a moment later. He unlatches it and holds it open for me. I reach out my hand to shake his. He looks startled but takes my hand in his. "It was nice meeting you," I say.

"It was nice meeting you too, Taviana," he answers and smiles.

Reluctantly, I let go of his hand and walk toward the road. I hear him close the gate behind me. I start off down the dirt road.

"Taviana?" he calls out.

I swing around, a stupid girlish hopefulness springing to life in my chest. "Yes?"

"You live with Celeste, don't you?"

That wasn't the question I expected to hear. "I do."

"Will you say hello to her from me?"

I stare at his earnest face a little too long, and he blushes and looks away. So the teenagers in this town aren't completely oblivious to each other after all. "Yeah, sure," I say, hoping I don't sound as disappointed as I feel.

"Thanks," he says, his head bobbing up and down.

"And I won't tell anyone about that either," I say.

He grins. "I knew I could trust you, Taviana," he says, and he turns and walks away.

I begin walking in the opposite direction, mulling over the realization that there is more going on in Unity than I was aware of.

Chapter Three

CELESTE

Daddy snatches up the tidy stack of shopping lists that have been delivered to us by various cousins this morning. It's his job to drive into Springdale each Saturday and purchase supplies for all our relatives in Unity.

I sit in a rocking chair with whimpering twin babies sprawled across my lap and observe Lena, Daddy's first wife. She's clearly restless and can't wait to get going. When she sees him take the lists, she tugs at the sash of her apron and hangs it on a hook by the door. Lena's the wife who always goes with Daddy to town. There's no point in his taking one of the others and flaunting the fact he has plural wives. The less we give them to talk about, the better.

But Daddy shocks us all this morning. He glances around the bustling room until he sees me, buried under babies. I meet his gaze, but after a moment I feel my face flush. Does he know about my impure rebellious thoughts? I begin humming to the twins and rock the chair more vigorously to settle them. Then, out of the blue, Daddy says, "Celeste will come with me today."

It takes me a moment to register the meaning of his words, but as soon as I do, I gather up the babies and hand them over to Nanette and Pam. I make eye contact with Mother, who is large with child again, sitting in an armchair, working her way through the mending basket. She pauses as she threads a needle and looks at me strangely. Is that sadness I read on her face? It doesn't matter. Nothing is going to keep me from spending a morning away from this noisy house. Before Daddy can change his mind, I, too, hang my apron on a hook and slide into a pair of outdoor shoes. I step around the dumbfounded Lena and follow my father out the door, allowing the springs to slam it shut behind me.

Sitting in the cab of Daddy's pickup truck, I marvel at my sudden good fortune. It's a fresh, sunny spring day. I have Daddy all to myself for a couple of hours. I'm away from the house, away from the never-ending chores and cranky, overburdened mothers, who are especially miserable on Saturday mornings when Lena gets to go to town with Daddy. Who knows how they'll feel today when he's chosen his oldest daughter over them. I refuse to think about the stares and rude remarks that are waiting for us in Springdale. The simple pleasure of getting away from Unity and all my younger siblings for a few hours is worth any amount of verbal abuse.

As we bump down the dirt road, I admire the wildflowers that line the ditch. And the sky! Has it ever been so blue? The mountains tower above us on one side of the road and farmland spreads out across the prairie on the other. We are the chosen people and this is clearly the chosen countryside.

"Celeste." Daddy's gravelly voice jolts me out of my dreamlike state. He isn't big on conversation, but that is what I love most about him. On those rare occasions when we are alone together, I'm free to lose myself in my own thoughts. That never happens at home, where any private thoughts get lost in the confusion of so many conversations all happening at once.

"Yes, Daddy?"

"I chose you to come with me today because there's something we need to talk about." He pauses, apparently looking for the right words. In that second, and with a sinking heart, I know exactly what's coming next.

"You'll be turning fifteen on your birthday."

"Yes, Daddy, I know."

"And as you know too, Celeste, daughters do not belong to their mothers or fathers. A daughter is only in her parents' keeping until the Elders have determined who she will be assigned to in marriage. Then you will belong to your husband for all eternity."

I nod but turn to stare out the window.

He continues. "The Prophet has begun asking for the Divine's guidance in determining who is to have you as a wife. Once you have turned fifteen, you can marry. I thought I'd remind you of that."

There is so much I want to say, but I don't say anything and Daddy doesn't say anything else either. I think he's just happy to have that off his chest. If he expected an argument from me, he isn't going to get it. Not today, anyway.

I keep my eyes on the passing scenery. Strangely, what had seemed like the makings of a perfect spring day now seem far less full of possibility. The wildflowers are just ugly weeds, and the glare of the sun is forcing me to squint.

OVER THE YEARS I've grown used to being stared at by the people in Springdale, but today I think it's me doing the most staring. It seems like everyone is out enjoying the first warm weekend of the season. Girls have gathered in groups on street corners, and there is a whole lot of skin showing. Belly button jewels sparkle in the sunlight, and there are all manner of tattoos. Boys and men are walking around without shirts and with shorts pulled down so low their underwear springs out the top. I find I don't know where to look, so, to cover my embarrassment, I just stare at my feet as I follow Daddy from store to store. He gathers the supplies and I trail after him, my arms laden down with packages and bags.

When we finish and everything is stowed in the cab of the truck, Daddy, who is a mechanic, goes off to talk business with some guys at the garage. He tells me he'll be back at the truck in an hour.

An hour? Normally I'd be delighted to have an hour all to myself, but what does he expect me to do in Springdale? It's too hot to wait in the parking lot.

Glancing around, I notice how many curious people there are, watching me. Already I've been asked by a nosy clerk if I'm one of Daddy's wives or his daughter. I decide it's best to get away from the center of town. The river that runs past Unity also runs right through a park at the south end of this town, and I decide to walk over there. Keeping my eyes down, I hurry away.

Unfortunately, the park is also crowded. Families have blankets spread out on the grassy slope, and picnic baskets lie open, filled with the kind of food you'd never see in Unity. There are empty junk-food wrappers being blown about in the breeze, and soda cans are bursting out of the top of the blue recycling bins. Dogs are romping together, and there are young people stretched out on towels, sunbathing, wearing practically nothing at all. Heat rises to my cheeks. Small children are playing at the water's edge. Even here, everyone stares at me. I turn upstream, hoping to find somewhere to be alone.

The river is high and loud with the spring runoff. Rounding a bend, I'm surprised to see another tower of rocks piled close to the water's edge. The beach is deserted here, so I wander over to take a closer look. I'm stunned by what I see. This is not another statue, but a selection of stones that have been balanced, precariously, one on top of the other. It's extraordinary that it doesn't topple over. Someone has clearly spent a lot of time setting the stones at just the right angles to make it work. The highest stone is standing with its widest part at the top, and its point is resting on a smaller stone beneath it, which is, in turn, balanced precariously on the tip of yet another stone, and so on. It looks so impossible that I reach out to see if it's been cemented together. I lift the top stone off and it comes free in my hand. Amazing. I carefully place it back the way I found it, but it falls off, and then, almost in slow motion, the whole tower crumbles. Shocked, I bend over and attempt to reassemble it, but one by one the stones drop back to the beach.

"That will be seven years of bad luck for you," a voice behind me says.

I whirl around and come face to face with a young man, his dark eyes shining. His chest is bare, and he's only wearing shorts. He crept up on me—I never heard a thing over the sound of the river.

"I'm sorry. I didn't mean to break it." I feel tears springing to my eyes. "I only wanted to see if it was cemented together." I gather up my dress and begin to run back toward the park.

"Hey, it's okay!" he yells. "I was just kidding! I'll build another one."

I glance back and see him standing there beside the fallen pile of stones, hands on his hips. From this distance, I realize that he's the same person I watched build the little statue near Unity. I turn and run even faster.

PULLING A WET apron from the laundry basket, I snap it hard and pass it to Taviana, who is hanging clothes on the line. My morning excursion into Springdale has left me jittery. "Do you believe in bad luck?" I ask her.

She regards me, a puzzled expression in her deep-set brown eyes. "I might have, before," she answers and takes the dress I'm passing to her.

"Before?"

"Before I came here," she says.

"Oh."

"Now I've learned, just like you have, that God determines what will happen to those who are faithful and obedient. It has nothing to do with luck."

"What about those who aren't faithful and obedient?"

She studies me again. "What's up, Celeste?"

I wonder how much to tell her. I can't get the image of those dark eyes and bare chest out of my head. There were wisps of hair on his chest. Do all men grow hair there? "Today, in Springdale," I tell her, "I accidentally broke something that belonged to a Gentile boy."

"You did?" Her eyebrows arch, trying to picture it.

I nod. "And he said I'd have seven years of bad luck."

Taviana's eyes light up and she laughs, hard, which I find reassuring. Clearly she doesn't believe I've been cursed. Dimples appear in her delicate, doll-like face, which is so different than the faces in our family. Except for Nanette, we tend to have broad foreheads, round cheeks and large blue eyes. When Taviana arrived, her dark hair was cropped short, and even though she's since let it grow out, it's still not nearly as long as ours, which has never been cut.

"Was it a mirror you broke?" she asks, turning back to the clothesline.

"No, why?"

"There's an old saying that if you break a mirror, you'll have seven years of bad luck."

"You will?"

She shrugs. "It's just an old saying."

"What other old sayings are there?"

"My mom had plenty. She said you'd have bad luck if you opened an umbrella in the house or if a black cat crossed your path. Walking under a ladder was also bad, unless, of course, you crossed your fingers."

"Did your mom believe these things?"

"She seemed to."

"And did you? Before you came here?"

She thinks about that. "Let's just say I didn't take any chances. I didn't walk under ladders or open umbrellas in the house."

We resume hanging the laundry. "So who was this Gentile boy?" she asks.

"I don't know. I saw this, this beautiful..." I shake my head, unable to find the right words. "This beautiful stone tower on the beach by the river." I'm getting excited just thinking about it again. "The stones were balanced on top of one another, but not like building blocks. These were balanced in such an interesting way, like on their pointed ends, and you'd swear they'd topple over, but they didn't."

"I remember seeing some of those on a beach once," Taviana muses. "They're like works of art, but so...so fragile.

And the builder has to just leave them there, to whatever may happen, like to people who—"

"Who destroy them!" I say, interrupting her. "I thought that maybe the stones were cemented together, so I lifted the top one off."

"Oh no!" she says.

"Oh yes. The whole tower collapsed."

"Oops."

"I hadn't seen anyone nearby, but suddenly this…this person—he was older than me but not a man—he was just standing there, behind me. He said that for breaking it I would have seven years of bad luck."

"You *have* been cursed!" Taviana declares.

"I have?"

She laughs again. "We don't believe in curses, Celeste."

"You're right." I hand her the last dress in the basket. "But still. I felt terrible."

"It goes with the territory," she says. "If he's going to build his art on a public beach, he has to know that it won't last."

"But it was so…so amazing," I tell her. "I didn't mean to break it."

"Get over it, Celeste," she tells me.

Get over it. I like these strange expressions Taviana has. I'm going to remember that one.

"And by the way," she adds. "I have a message for you."

"You do?"

"Yep. Guess who it's from?"

My mind is blank. "I have no idea."

"I'll give you a hint. He's cute. He has brown hair and a really nice smile."

I feel my skin burn. Can it be? I gather up the laundry basket and the clothes-pegs, hoping she won't notice my skin.

"I have no idea," I tell her.

"Really?" she asks, looking sly.

"Taviana. Just tell me what the message is."

"Okay," she teases. "The message is he says hello."

"Who is 'he'?" I push the back door open and enter the house, pretending not to be too interested in her message.

"C'mon," she says. "Give me your top three guesses."

"Taviana!" I say. "I have no idea."

"Okay," she says. "Another hint." She's whispering now because there are so many people about. "It's another guy, older than you, but not a man."

I glare at her. We're immersed in family noise again, multiple conversations, sister wives barking commands at older children, crying and commotion all around us.

"Celeste!" my sister Rebecca squeals. She has seen me come in, has run over and wrapped her chubby four-year-old arms around my legs. "Can you play with me now? Please?"

I stroke her soft hair. Rebecca and I share the same mother and the same birthday, so I think of us as having a special connection. She seems to think so too, always coming to me for things before she goes to one of the mothers or even Nanette. "What do you want to do?" I ask her.

"Let's color pictures," she says.

"Good idea." I glance back at Taviana, irritated with her silly game. She makes eye contact with me, and there's a little smile on her lips. She mouths the word I've hoped all along she'll say. "Jon."

I take Rebecca's hand in mine and guide her to the shelf in the living room where the coloring books with pictures of bible stories are stored. I don't look back at Taviana. I can't let her see how happy I am.

$\mathcal{N}anette$

"C eleste," I whisper in the dark. "Why did Father take you to Springdale?"

I've been waiting all day to speak with her alone. When I came in from the garden this afternoon, I saw her playing with Rebecca, and she looked...different. Her cheeks were flushed pink, and the two of them were giggling and whispering in each other's ears. Giggling is not something Celeste does. We peeled potatoes and scrubbed vegetables together before dinner, but there were too many people in the kitchen to have a private conversation. Still, even while scraping carrots, I noticed that her frown was gone, and she even offered to feed the babies. Something good must have happened.

Celeste flips over to face me in our bed. She doesn't answer right away, so I prod a little more. "You seemed so happy all evening."

Now she sighs. "Daddy just told me that I'll soon be assigned to a husband."

"You already knew that."

"I guess it was a reminder."

"So, are you excited?"

"No, Nanette. I'm not."

"Why not?"

"I'm just not. I'm not ready. We've talked about this."

"When will you be ready?"

She hesitates. "Maybe never."

"Celeste! That's blasphemy."

"Nanette," Celeste whispers. "Have you ever wondered what it would be like to be with boys your own age?"

"No."

"I wonder about it," she says.

"Shh!" I tell her, and I cringe. I don't want to hear this, especially from my own sister.

She ignores me. "And I wonder what it would be like to select my own husband, someone I love."

I cover my ears with my hands. How can she say these things? "No more!" I tell her. "You know as I do that we must practice purity." A surge of anger rips through me. I struggle to keep my voice quiet, yet I must remind her of what she knows so well. "You'll never attain eternal life if you keep thinking those thoughts," I whisper into her face. She flips away and pulls the covers over her head. I yank them back off and continue. "Accepting the hand of the Lord in deciding our marriages is the most sacred principle of all, and plural marriage is the only way to salvation!" I feel like I'm the Prophet himself, standing at the pulpit. Passion surges through me as I consider my next point.

Celeste groans noisily, pulling the blankets back over her head, and then one of our little sisters in another bed begins to whine. That sets off a whole chorus of whimpering and crying, so I swallow my anger, climb out of our bed and go to them one at a time, stroking their heads, shushing them. Celeste doesn't get up to help, and her back is still turned to me when I finally return to bed. Tonight I'm glad for that. I turn my back to her too.

I GO THROUGH the motions of helping get everyone ready for church service in the morning, but today it's a huge effort. Lying awake last night, I was troubled by thoughts about both Taviana and Celeste, and today my heart and head are weary. I know I should report Celeste's impure thoughts to Father, as well as Taviana's behavior with the apostates, but I don't want either of them to be punished. And yet, how else will they be saved? Taviana, I think, will be okay. She was once a Gentile, she didn't know better, but she is learning, and she mostly tries hard to fit in. I truly believe we have saved her. Celeste, on the other hand, has been born and raised in The Movement. Where do her impure thoughts come from? Why does she challenge the sacred principles? She's just making herself miserable, and now she's making me miserable too, and scared, worrying about what will become of her.

My father, his four wives and all their children fill up the last three pews in the church. I generally spend the service focused on keeping the younger children quiet, but today I'm startled when the Prophet begins to speak earnestly about plural marriage. It's as if he heard our conversation last night, and I glance at Celeste to see if she is also amazed at the coincidence. But Celeste appears preoccupied, and I see her glancing about the sanctuary, as if she's looking for someone.

"Fathers and Mothers," the Prophet bellows over the noise of fussy babies, "from the time your daughter can crawl, you must teach her that she does not belong to you but to the Prophet and the man the Prophet will assign her to in marriage. Only these men, and I mean men, not boys, can take your daughters to the highest degree of the celestial kingdom where they will be queens and priestesses."

I think about the Prophet's twenty-six wives and more than ninety children, who make up a large chunk of our community. He has a lot of daughters to teach this lesson to.

Now he takes a deep breath, and his intense hawklike eyes scan the congregation. "When the Lord assigns me a new wife," he roars, "I take her into my bedroom, I remove all her clothes and I seize any worldly possessions she has arrived with. I then dress her in clothes that I have had prepared for her and send everything else back to her mother and father. My wife then knows that she belongs only to me for all eternity, and she no longer has connections to her mother and father. This is the only way a man can achieve oneness in his kingdom." His fist slams the pulpit.

The Prophet continues his impassioned sermon, but my mind wanders. I visualize standing there alone with him, his hands undressing me, one garment at a time. My heart races, and my palms feel sticky. I don't know if this is because the image frightens me or excites me. Maybe both.

As soon as the service is over, I see Celeste slip out the front door. I hope she has listened carefully and is feeling remorseful. I help my mother steer the children downstairs to the playroom for the social hour. Then I settle Mother in a chair beside Uncle Jeremy's wife, Colleen, who is also heavy with child. When I'm sure she's comfortable, I hurry over to the table where my assignment is to ladle out juice.

It's a warm morning and the mugs of juice disappear as fast as I can fill them. When the initial rush has ended, I take a small break and wipe my hands on my apron. Looking up, I notice Martin Nielsson standing by the table, watching me. He has become a regular Sunday morning visitor at my table.

"Hello, Nanette," he says.

"Hello, Mr. Nielsson." I lower my eyes and busy myself with wiping up the spills on the table.

"It was an especially inspiring service today, wasn't it?"

I nod but don't say anything. It's unusual for an elder to strike up a conversation with a child outside of his own family, especially a girl child, and I haven't yet figured out how to respond to this man.

"You're looking so grown-up today, Nanette," he says.

I have even less idea how to respond to that. I busy myself filling more mugs with juice.

"How old are you now, child?" he asks.

"Thirteen."

"Ahh. Not long before the Prophet will be awaiting guidance from the Lord to determine who you will belong to forevermore."

"My sister, Celeste, she will be married first," I say. Now I find the courage to look directly at him, and I notice the crinkles around his light blue eyes and the gray streaks that run through his hair. He must be about the same age as Daddy, but much, much more handsome.

"Ah yes. Celeste." He looks about the room. "And where is Celeste today?"

"She's here somewhere," I tell him, hoping that I'm not telling a lie.

"And how about Taviana? Will she become a wife to someone soon?"

"I don't know. I don't think the Prophet has decided what to do with her."

"Yes, she is an unusual case."

I can feel him studying me some more. "You have grown very lovely, Nanette," he says.

My face burns.

"Well then, I'll be seeing you around," he says, bowing slightly. He turns and walks away. I watch as he gathers up his five wives and their children. He seems kind and gentle, joking with the children, putting his arm around each wife in turn as he steers the group toward the door.

Is he wondering what it would be like to have me as a celestial wife? I feel an odd pang inside. I will miss living with my mother and Daddy and my brothers and sisters, but I'm ready to make that leap from child to wife. I long to sleep in the arms of the man God chooses for me, and I want to feel the stirring of a baby deep inside. Perhaps I should speak to Daddy, convince him that I am ready to serve God by being an obedient wife. Maybe the Prophet can make an exception and listen to God's direction for me at the same time he listens for Celeste.

Celeste. How can she not see the beauty in celestial marriage? She is even named for it.

Mr. Nielsson has finished gathering his family and is trailing out the door behind them. He turns at the last moment and glances at me once more. Our eyes meet, and he smiles. I return the smile but abruptly turn away as I remember the image the Prophet described during this morning's sermon, the image of him undressing his new wives in his bedroom. A bead of sweat tickles as it meanders down my back. I look up one more time and find Mr. Nielsson still studying me.

Please God. Assign me to Mr. Nielsson.

AT SCHOOL ON Monday, I spend the day assisting Sarah Waring, our teacher, with the first-grade children. In small groups I have them print the letters of the alphabet on the chalkboard, and then I listen to them recite short passages from the children's version of The Book. Sarah doesn't feel I need to study any further, yet it is the law that I remain in school for another year, so I mostly help with the teaching. This arrangement suits me just fine.

Celeste has finished the required amount of schooling and now stays home each day and works alongside our mother and Taviana. Taviana mostly helps with the babies, and Celeste does laundry, gardening and kitchen work. Mother is having a difficult time with her current pregnancy, so Taviana will remain with us until Mother is better, or until after the baby has been born. Then Jacob may assign her to another family or perhaps even to a husband. No one knows for sure.

I think about Taviana and the boys from the other night. Sometimes she seems so close to reverting to her old ways, yet I know she likes it here and wants to stay. I wonder if it's because Celeste has spent so much time with her that she is questioning our traditions. That is something else I could talk to Daddy about.

At three o'clock, Celeste meets me at the school to take the children to the playground. We haven't spoken to each other since she shared her impure thoughts in bed the other night, and now she lags behind as I lead the children toward the play area. I notice that she's not making eye contact with me, which is fine. I'm still angry with her too. She will bring shame on Father and our entire family if she continues thinking as she does.

As we pass the Nielsson compound, I see that the usual pack of Nielsson boys are working on fence repairs again, but today they seem more orderly, more focused. I take a closer look and notice that Mr. Nielsson is working alongside them. Seeing him gives me a start, and I find myself checking that my apron is straight and that my hair hasn't tugged free of its braid. When he sees us passing, he rests for a moment, wipes his brow with a handkerchief that he pulls from a back pocket, and gives a little wave in our direction. I swallow my excitement, nod my head and carry on with the children, trying not to read too much into this encounter. I glance back at Celeste, wondering if she's noticed Mr. Nielsson's gesture, and see that she too is smiling, but not in the direction of Mr. Nielsson, who is standing near the barn, but at the boys who are closer to the road.

I believe I will have to talk to Daddy about her after all.

WHEN THE DISHES are done and the smallest children have been settled, I slip out the back door and begin my search for Daddy, hoping that neither Deborah or Lena see me. I know he often goes to the barn in the evenings. He has converted it into an automotive shop. We're discouraged from disturbing him, but I think this time I need to make an exception. The coast seems to be clear. I cross the yard, and as I enter the cool darkness of the barn, I hear him humming in a room that was once the tack room but is now his office. I knock softly at the door, not wanting to startle him. He looks up from the papers he is sorting and is surprised to see me. "Nanette," he says. "Is something the matter? Is your mother...?"

"Everything's fine, Daddy," I assure him. "Mother is resting, and Taviana is watching the children."

"Oh," he says, clearly puzzled but relieved at the same time. "Then what is it?"

"I was wondering if…if I could talk to you for a few minutes," I say.

"Certainly, Nanette." He leans back in his chair and folds his hands across his ample stomach. "What is it you wish to talk about?"

"Um, two things." I clear my throat. "First of all…" Oh no. Even though I've rehearsed the words I want to say to him all afternoon, my mind is suddenly blank and my mouth is dry.

He watches me struggle. "Are you having trouble at school, Nanette?" he asks.

"No, school is fine. But the fact is, Daddy…" I remember what I've come to him about and I summon up my courage. "I feel ready to become a wife and mother. I live obediently, I have perfect faith. I want you to ask the Prophet to determine who I'm to spend eternity with."

"But, Nanette," my father says, "you're only—"

"Thirteen. I know. But I'm older than my years, Daddy. And I'm pure of thought and spirit. I truly wish to move forward with God's plan for me."

"It is against the laws of our country, Nanette…"

"Having plural wives is against the law of our country too, Daddy. But we have our own laws here, the laws of our Heavenly Father, and I know that I am ready to be a wife."

"I'm waiting to hear who Celeste will marry," he tells me.

"I know. But that's another thing, Daddy."

"What's another thing?"

"Celeste. She is…she's not pure of thought." I immediately feel guilty for tattling on her, but I continue anyway. "Unlike me," I tell him, "she feels she is not ready to be married. And," I add, lowering my voice, "she secretly covets boys her own age."

"She does?"

"Yes. And she wishes to choose her own husband. I wonder if this could be Taviana's influence."

Daddy stares at me. "And you, Nanette? Do you wish this too?"

"Of course not, Daddy!" I say, then add, "Although I think Martin Nielsson may fancy me as a prospective wife."

His expression changes abruptly. "Has he done something inappropriate?"

"Oh no. He just passes pleasantries with me after the church service."

Daddy rubs his chin, thinking about this. "The Lord will reveal who you will marry in His own good time, but you must be patient."

"I know. I'm not sure why I mentioned it."

"And I know Taviana is working hard to fit in here. Your mother needs her right now. But I will talk with her."

I nod. A talking-to from Daddy may be all Taviana needs.

"Thank you for coming to speak to me," he says. "I will

do as you request and speak to the Prophet. I will also speak with your sister."

"Thank you." I walk around the desk and wrap my arms around him in a hug. At first he is stiff, awkward, but after a moment he hugs me back.

"You've been a wonderful daughter, Nanette."

"Thanks." I smile at him. "And you've been a wonderful father."

Daddy blinks hard and returns to his paperwork. I slip back across the field and into the sprawling house.

Chapter Five

CELESTE

Receiving the message that Jon said hello sent me into spasms of joy on Saturday afternoon. I felt like a small girl again instead of a soon-to-be overburdened sister wife and potential mother. Playing with Rebecca actually became fun, and I didn't resent cooking and cleaning up after the entire family. Even Deborah, Daddy's third wife, who loves to boss me about, didn't annoy me. Nanette came close to it with her lecture about celestial marriages, but I was back to feeling joyful Sunday morning.

I looked for Jon in church, and when I saw him he smiled quickly, so as not to be noticed by anyone, but it was definitely meant for me. I thought I was going to burst with happiness. I kept looking in his direction, and the next time our eyes met, I smiled right back. An elbow jabbed me in the ribs and I glanced at Taviana, who winked. Thank goodness it was Taviana who'd spotted our smiling exchange, and not Nanette. I elbowed her back.

I didn't hear a word the Prophet said, even though I knew he was ranting and raving about something. Instead I marveled at the invisible flow of energy that seemed to pull Jon and me together despite all the resistance around us. I wondered if he felt the same pull.

When the service ended, I was desperate to stay physically close to Jon. I decided to skip the social hour downstairs and go directly outside. If asked, I'd say it was to enjoy some fresh air, but really I wanted to watch the boys as they kicked a ball around.

I wandered around the church garden, admiring the cheerful daffodils. The tulips were straining toward the sun, their petals still closed tight, but I noticed they were practically trembling as they prepared to explode into bloom.

The boys were playing their usual game of soccer in the field, and I knew that Jon would be among them. When I took my eyes off the flowers to glance over at the boys, I saw that Jon had noticed me. He'd lingered behind the pack of boys who were running away from the church in pursuit of the ball. We stared at each other for a moment, my heart pounding in my chest. He jogged backwards, still watching me, but then turned to catch up with the pack. I returned to my stroll, allowing my mind to wander. I wondered, what would I say to Jon if I actually had the chance to have a conversation with him? What would he say to me? I doubted that he had perfect faith, like Nanette. If he did, he wouldn't have smiled at me. I might ask him if he intends to stay in Unity. So many of our boys leave.

Wham! The ball smacked into the side of the building and rolled to a stop under a bush. I jumped back, surprised, and then found myself face to face with Jon, who was there to retrieve it. I'd never stood that close to him, and I could actually feel the heat radiating from his body. He was panting, hard, and I found that his sweaty male scent excited me.

"Meet me at the river, near the playground, tomorrow after dinner," he whispered while digging the ball out of the shrubs with his toe.

"I don't know..."

"Just come when you can," he urged. "I'll watch for you." He kicked the ball back to the waiting players. With a final glance at me, he jogged away. As I watched him run off, I wondered if he'd kicked the ball here on purpose or if it was just a lucky coincidence.

I returned to my stroll around the garden but I no longer saw the flowers. Instead I marveled at how beautiful Jon's face was. My heart pounded in a chest churning with anticipation, anxiety, excitement, fear. I felt fully alive.

The rest of Sunday dragged by. I'd never known one day to last so long. One moment I was determined to meet Jon at the river, and the next I knew that I absolutely couldn't. I tossed all night, remembering how he smelled and how warm the light in his eyes was.

On Monday I led the children past the Nielsson farm again. This time, when Jon smiled at me, I knew I'd find a way to meet with him.

I BEGIN WATCHING for my opportunity to escape as soon as the dinner dishes are done. When the littlest ones have been put to bed, I grab the bucket of scraps we collect for the compost. Just as I step onto the back stoop, I see a movement near the barn. A body slips inside, a body that looks suspiciously like Nanette. Why would she be going into the barn? To talk to Daddy, I suppose, but about what? Not about me, I hope.

I dump the compost scraps onto the heap, use a pitchfork to turn the pile and then start back toward the house. The evening is warm and fragrant. I walk slowly, enjoying it, and then I realize that this is my opportunity to disappear. Nanette would be the first to notice my absence, but she's absent herself. Others will have seen me leave with the compost bucket, but it may take a while for anyone to notice that I haven't returned. I leave the bucket by the back door, turn and walk briskly through the garden and out the gate. I don't look back.

My stomach clenches, and I fully expect to hear someone call my name, ordering me back, but no one does. Our neighbors will just think I've been sent on an errand. As I walk past the Nielsson farm, I'm tempted to slow down so Jon has a better chance to see me, but I don't. My heart is hammering so hard in my chest that I'm afraid it will explode. I cut through the playground and turn toward the river. Rounding the first bend, hoping to be out of sight of any people passing by, I find a place near the trees where I can still see the playground, and Jon when he approaches, but where I'll also be camouflaged by the trees.

Collapsing to the ground, I take deep breaths, trying to slow my breathing and heart rate. I close my eyes, then open them and scan the riverbanks.

Is that what I think it is? I scramble to my feet, hike my skirt up and dash across the beach. Sure enough, the first statue is still standing there, as is the one I built, but now there is a third rock man. Once again he looks like the first two but completely different as well. My heart swells at the thought of the boy coming back, seeing my creation and deciding to add to it. We're building a community.

I look back to where I've come from but don't see any signs of Jon. Once again I tuck the hem of my skirt into my apron and start scouring the beach for appropriate stones. I've put the legs and torso in place when I see him in the distance. He has also seen me and is coming over to where I'm working. I quickly pull my hem back out of my apron and smooth my dress down. What will he think of me, building rock people, my dress hiked up, exposing my legs?

An attack of shyness hits me as Jon approaches. What am I doing here? What was I thinking? I haven't been alone with a boy since I was a little girl. My mouth goes dry.

"Hi, Celeste," Jon says. He looks right at me. "I'm glad you could get away for a while."

I look down at my feet, then back at him. I see a glint of mischief in his eyes, and I have to smile. The shyness begins to evaporate. "I'm glad I could too." We look directly at each other for a moment, and I now know for sure that I wasn't imagining the flow of energy that was drawing us together in church. It is encircling us now, and I feel a mad fluttering of little wings deep inside. Can this be normal?

"What are you making?" he asks, noticing the rock statues.

I quickly explain how I discovered the first one a few days ago, built another one to keep the first one company and found that a third one had been added since then. I show him the one I'm working on.

"So now you just need the arms, the neck and a head," he says.

I smile again, pleased that he didn't make fun of me for doing this. "Yeah," I say. "Want to help?"

He pauses, considering. Uh-oh. Maybe I was wrong. Maybe he does think this is a stupid thing to do.

"I'd like to make my own," he says.

Now I really am going to explode with happiness. "Great idea!"

We separate, looking for stones that please us. It's a little harder for me now as I'm back to tripping over my dress, but I finally get mine finished. I stand back, admiring my work. Jon is arranging arms on his. I watch him trying different stones, but, not satisfied, he tosses them aside and searches for better ones. When the arms are done, he adds a couple of flat stones for a neck and then places an almost round stone on top, the head. It's balanced so perfectly it reminds me of the rock tower I saw in Springdale, the one I destroyed.

Jon moves over to stand with me and we study the finished products. The five statues are each different heights, their body parts are of various shapes, but they still all manage to look related. And cheery. Jon steps forward and fiddles with the arm on his. When he steps back again, I see what he's done. One arm on his statue is reaching out to touch an arm on mine, giving the impression that they are holding hands. I pray my knees don't buckle.

THE SUN HAS set and it's getting darker. Jon and I have moved into the shadow of the trees, where we've found a patch of moss to sit on.

"I got your message from Taviana," I tell him.

"I figured you had," he says.

The silence between us becomes awkward. There's so much to say, but it's so hard to know where to start.

"I'm going to have to think of a good explanation for where I've been tonight," I tell him.

He nods sympathetically. "Maybe Taviana will cover for you."

"Maybe." Nanette certainly won't.

"Celeste," he says and hesitates. Then he takes a deep breath. "Do you ever question your faith, or the ways of our Movement?"

I nod. "If I didn't, I wouldn't be here right now."

"That's what I figured," he says, almost sadly. "It's hard, though, isn't it?"

"Hard?"

"Yeah, it would be easier to have perfect faith. My brother, Simon, he's like that. He accepts everything, and he's so untroubled. It makes him feel good to fulfill the Prophet's commands."

I hear myself sigh. "My sister, Nanette, she's like that too."

"My brother, he'll grow old here," he continues. "He'll prove his faith to the Prophet, and he'll be assigned numerous wives." Now Jon sighs too.

I look over at him in the dimming light. The mischievous look has gone from his eyes, and now they're filled with a deep sadness.

"I've talked to some guys who've left Unity," he tells me.

"You have?" I hope the alarm that I feel doesn't show in my voice.

He nods.

All the exhilaration of the day melts completely away. I know there's no place for Jon in my future, but I still want him nearby.

"What about you?" he asks.

"Me?"

"Yeah. Do you ever think of leaving?"

The question surprises me. Girls don't leave Unity. Where would we go? We're too young to get jobs, and by the time we're old enough, we're married with babies. A few older women have fled in the night with their children, but often the children find their way home to live with their fathers and other mothers. "No," I tell him. "Though I wish I could, before I'm assigned to a husband."

We sit in silence again. Jon reaches to pick up an odd-shaped stone lying on the beach, and his hand accidentally brushes my arm. A tremor rushes right through me.

"It's an arrowhead!" he exclaims.

"A what?" I ask, trying to settle my heart again.

"An arrowhead. The First Nations people chiseled them from stone and attached them to the ends of their arrows."

"Oh." I have no comment to make about arrowheads.

"Maybe it's up to us to change things," he says, still examining the stone.

"Change things?" I ask. "Like what?"

He regards me. "You can refuse to be assigned to a husband."

"If I did that I'd be banished from Unity. I'd be an apostate. Then what would become of me?"

"You could move to Springdale, finish high school and get work. Maybe even have a career."

I study his face, amazed. "Think of the shame I'd bring on my family! And who would I live with?"

Jon just shrugs. "We have choices, even if they're not easy ones."

"Maybe you do," I tell him. "But I don't know anyone who would take me in. And besides, I love my parents, all of them, and my brothers and sisters, even though they drive me crazy. I'd miss them."

"So," he says, "you question your faith, but you're not prepared to do anything about it." He pushes the arrowhead into my hands.

I don't answer.

"Then I guess you will have to settle for being a plural wife," he tells me.

It's almost completely dark now, but Jon's face is close enough to mine that I can see him gazing intently at me. I look away. His words hurt, like he's criticizing me. Some small part of me knows he's right, but it's too hard to think about it. "I better go," I say, but I don't move.

Now I feel his hand on my chin and he turns my face to look at him. "Just think about it, Celeste. You came here tonight. That's a start." Then, before I know it, his lips are on mine. For the briefest of seconds I stay put, savoring the wave of heat that surges through me, but then I push him away, jump to my feet and start running down the beach toward the road.

"Celeste!" I hear Jon call out, but he doesn't try to catch me. I keep running.

Chapter Six

Taviana

The evening is just beginning to darken. My chores are done and I have nothing else to do, so I decide to take a walk. I haven't been able to find Celeste anywhere, and Nanette has been ignoring me ever since I stopped to talk to the boys at the Nielsson farm the other night. As I pull on my shoes, I consider walking in that direction again. It's not that I'm looking for trouble, but chatting with the boys would make the evening a little less dull.

It's at times like this that I miss TV and videos. I never had a computer, but I liked going to the library and mucking about on one of theirs. I had a Hotmail account for a while, but I didn't have anyone to write to, so I quit checking it. Celeste loves hearing about all the things you can discover with a computer and the Internet. It's strange to think she's never used one or watched a TV. It's even stranger to think that if I stay here, I may never use either of them again.

The beam of headlights swinging into the long driveway startles me. Peering into the twilight, I recognize the car as a police cruiser, and at that same moment I hear the patter of running footsteps. Spinning about, I catch a glimpse of a small figure flying through the garden and racing toward the house. My old instincts kick in, and I melt back into the doorway, my heart racing. A panicky voice shouts from the back step. "Taviana! Hide, now!"

Celeste's dad, Kelvin, materializes from behind a bedroom door, buttoning up his shirt. His eyes are wide, frightened. He's always so totally in control that it alarms me even more to see him like this. He grabs my arm and pulls me toward the stairs that lead to the basement. I stumble down behind him and watch as he unlatches a deadbolt and yanks open the door that leads under the house into a cold storage area where vegetables and jars of preserves are kept over the winter. Goosebumps bubble up on my arms when I'm hit by the cool dank air. I peer in and see that the dirt floor is mostly bare, the food being used up by this time of year. There's a single unlit lightbulb hanging from the ceiling, and the crawl space is about four feet high. I can't see the back wall, but the tunnel-shaped room appears to go a long way under the house.

Before Kelvin even says anything, I shake my head, hard, and back away. I know he wants me to go in there but there's no way.

"Go as far back as you can," he whispers, pushing me forward. He's so anxious he doesn't even realize that I'm resisting, or if he does, he doesn't care. I duck and reach to pull the chain dangling from the lightbulb, but he bats my hand away. "Leave it!" he orders, and then, with a final push, I'm in the room, the door closes and I hear the latch slide into place. My world goes black, and the cold seeps under my skin.

Reaching out to where the door should be, I feel for a handle, but there is nothing on this side. I shove it with my shoulder, but it doesn't budge. A shudder runs through me, my mouth opens to scream, but then I hear the clatter of heels on the floor above my head. Male voices are raised in anger, but I can't make out the words.

I clamp my mouth shut and swallow the panic. Hunching over, I try to do as he said, but my head keeps cracking on the low ceiling. Getting down on my hands and knees, I attempt to crawl, but my stupid dress makes that impossible. I tuck the hem into my apron and creep forward on my hands and knees, like an animal. Deeper and deeper I go into the darkness. When my head smacks against the far wall, I sit down and rest my back against it, drawing my knees up to my chest. I circle them tight with my arms and drop my head. Something tickles my cheek and I swat at it. Was it a spider? I shudder again.

A wave of claustrophobic panic threatens to undo me, but I clench my jaw, knowing that something serious is happening upstairs and I have to remain calm. In my old life, when I was first living on the streets, an experienced girl taught me a technique for making the time with customers go by faster. I learned to detach my mind from my body, and I'd travel to faraway, exotic places. I imagined hot sand between my toes on a white sand beach in Mexico, the burning heat of the sun scorching my skin, or the cold slap of wind as I cycled through the foothills in Nepal. My adventures were endless, and each day I searched the Internet for more and more places to travel to in my mind. Maybe it will work here too. I hunker down, letting my mind drift.

The down quilt covering me is thick but weightless. I sink back into the fluffy pillows and gaze out the window at the snowcapped mountain peaks of the Swiss Alps. I stroke the Saint Bernard dog who is lounging on the bed beside me, panting happily. I press my forehead to his and scratch him behind the ears, not even minding his doggy breath. If he were a cat he'd be purring. I am safe, warm and loved. There is food to eat and family to hang with…

A sudden stomp on the floor over my head snaps me back to the present. The angry voices are still at it in the room over my head. I try to find my way back to that imaginary bed in the cozy room, but I've begun to shiver and I find I'm no longer able to detach. What is going on upstairs?

I squeeze my knees even tighter to my chest. I thought the police had given up on me. We first got to know one another when I was just a little girl, living with my mom. Social workers used to arrive on a regular basis, sometimes to take me to foster care and sometimes to check on our living conditions. I realize now that even though she was into drugs and hadn't a clue about how to bring up a kid, Mom loved me like crazy, so she raised hell at the sight of them. I was all she had and she didn't want to lose me.

She'd push me behind her and throw pots and pans at the social workers, swearing her head off. They began bringing police protection with them. By the time I was twelve, I no longer waited for the social workers to rescue me from her. I'd begun running away from home, and the situation reversed. The police began returning me to her.

There's only so many ways for a thirteen-year-old girl on her own to survive, and it seems there's nothing you can't get used to after a time. That's when the police started dragging me to group homes, and then juvie jail, but the situation never changed. As soon as I was released, I was right back on the streets. It was the only thing I knew how to do. I couldn't make it in school. I was too different from the other kids, and they never failed to remind me of that.

Everything changed when I met Jacob. At first I thought he was just another customer, but he only wanted to take me out for lunch once a week when he came to town to pick up a load of fertilizer. After a time I grew to trust him. He began telling me about Unity, and it sounded like a nice place with everyone working together for the common good. Despite that, I don't think I would have agreed to come with him if it weren't for the close call...

My shivering turns to shudders and I squeeze my eyes tight. I've been able to forget this horror, until now...

He was going to murder me. In sickening detail he described how he was going to do it...carving my naked body with his hunting knife...slowly getting deeper...nicking my organs. The pain would be severe, but not so severe that I'd pass out and escape the torture. He said that I would pay for my sins as the

SISTER WIFE

*others had done before me, starting with his mother. There was
nothing I could do, my hands were tied behind my back. I had to
listen to him, my stomach a huge cramp as his car hurtled down
the highway.*

*And then the doe was there...in the center of the highway...
her eyes large in the car headlights. It was as if time stood still
for a moment, the deer looking directly at me, telling me she
was there to protect me. He slammed on the brakes, swerved to
miss her, lost control and hit a tree instead. It knocked us both
out cold, and when I awoke I was in the emergency room of the
hospital. The man had disappeared as soon as he came to, and I
snuck out before social services got involved.*

I saw Jacob the next day and he asked about the bruises
on my face. I told him about the doe, and he looked at me
with awe and said I must be one of the chosen ones. That
God put that doe there to save me.

I wouldn't have bought into it but I couldn't get the
eyes of that doe out of my mind. She really did appear to
be sending me a message, and in the state I was in, I was
willing to believe it was a message from God. So when Jacob
once again invited me to come here, I gladly agreed. I knew
I couldn't do that work again anyway, and I had nothing
to lose. I convinced myself that I would be happy living
here, even if it was so old-fashioned. Maybe God truly was
looking out for me, and putting Jacob in my life was His
way to keep me safe. No more cold nights on the streets.
No more arrests. And for the most part I have been content.

Heavy footsteps bang down the stairs. I curl up as small
as I can and squeeze my eyes shut. I hear the latch being

unfastened and the door creaks open. Holding my breath, I will myself to be invisible.

I don't dare open my eyes, but even with them shut, I know the beam of a flashlight is exploring the crawl space. Am I far enough back? A throat clears and feet shuffle on the floor. Have they discovered me? Just when I think I can't hold my breath another second, the light blinks off, throwing me back into pitch-blackness, and the door is yanked shut. My breath escapes in a whoosh.

The feet clomp up the stairs and I don't hear any more voices. It feels like forever until I hear the sound of car tires scraping along the gravel driveway again. A moment later a single set of footsteps descends the stairs and the door opens.

"Taviana, you can come out."

My arms and legs have cramped up, but I struggle toward the light. My knee traps my dress under me and I hear it rip. Kelvin offers me a hand when I reach the door. Blinking in the bright light, I stiffly follow him back up the stairs and into the kitchen, where his wives and some of the older children have congregated. Nanette is there but, just like everyone else, she avoids making eye contact with me. All their faces are serious and no one is talking. Even Celeste's mom, Irene, is here, which is surprising as she's on complete bed rest now. It's Irene who gives me a mug of herbal tea and a sympathetic look. I accept the tea gratefully. I'm cold, right down to my core.

"I guess you know that we just had a visit from the police, Taviana," Kelvin says to me. He lowers himself into a chair at the head of the large table and motions for me to take one.

I nod and carry on rubbing my arms with my hands. I feel a shawl being draped over my shoulders and turn to see Irene stepping away.

"They accused us of keeping you here against your will," he tells me.

"That's not true," I say. "I could leave anytime I want."

He nods. "And I appreciate all the help you've given my wives, especially now, with Irene's condition being what it is."

Irene and I make eye contact, and she smiles warmly again. I do my best to smile back.

"The trouble is," Kelvin continues, "our small community needs to keep a very low profile in the greater world. The laws of this country conflict with the laws of our faith, but because we keep to ourselves and don't cause any trouble, we are left alone."

I had wondered how they got away with the plural wife thing.

"We are also protected by laws that entitle us to religious freedom, to practice our faith."

There's a banging at the front door and we all jump in unison. Deborah makes eye contact with Kelvin, and he nods. She leaves the kitchen. I can feel the increased tension in the room as we wait to see who's there. A moment later, Jacob and the Prophet enter the room, followed by Deborah.

Jacob's eyes meet mine, and I see the concern in them. "Are you okay?" he asks.

I just nod.

Kelvin is standing again, clearly anxious at finding the Prophet in his home.

"Good evening, sir."

"Clearly it has not been a good evening," the Prophet replies. He glances about the room but stops when he sees me. I watch as he sizes me up. "I would ask, please, that we be left alone with only the men and this one girl." His eyes are still fixed on me.

Kelvin nods. "Ladies, children, off you go."

The room clears and the Prophet and Jacob join Kelvin and me at the table. I want to drink my tea, yet I feel it might be rude in their presence. I wrap my cold hands around the warm mug instead.

"The police came to my home first tonight," the Prophet says, "accusing us of harboring this…this runaway."

I feel my face burn, and I drop my gaze to my lap.

"Apparently some boys from Highrock reported talking with her here late one evening."

Uh-oh.

"I told them I knew nothing about a runaway," he continues, "but they snooped about until some innocent child revealed where she was living. I saw one of my boys hightail it over here to warn you, and I'm assuming he arrived in time."

"Yes, sir, he did," Kelvin says.

"Kelvin," the Prophet continues, "I clearly had a lapse in judgment when I agreed to let this girl live here. I don't need to explain to you why we can't be drawing attention to Unity, especially police attention. Surely you remember what happened in '92, when all our children were dragged from their beds in the night and taken to Springdale? Reporters and police officers descended upon our little community, and our faith became the target of vicious accusations. Pictures of us were splashed on the front pages of newspapers right across the nation. It's taken us years to put that event behind us and carry on living the simple peaceful life we strive for."

"I remember it well," Kelvin says.

"So the question is," the Prophet says, "why are we tempting a repeat of that event by harboring a runaway in our community?"

For a man who is supposed to be so great and wise and the channel through which God speaks to us, he sure is insensitive. I've been treated like family here and don't appreciate being called a "runaway."

"Excuse me, sir," Jacob says, stepping into the conversation and rescuing Kelvin. "It is I who brought Taviana to Unity. I found her living on the streets, and she told me a story that led me to believe she's one of God's chosen people. I could see that she needed a safe and caring place to live. You may not realize it, sir, but Taviana has been a good and obedient member of our community. She works hard at whatever task she is given."

Kelvin takes it up from there. "Taviana has been a contributing member in my home over the past few months. My wife Irene is struggling in her current condition, and Taviana has been a tremendous help to her."

"That may well be," the Prophet says, "but because of her, the police are now questioning our traditions again. Tonight one of them said that they 'know' of things that go on in this town. I did not like the tone of his voice or what he was implying. I cannot allow this girl to continue living among us and drawing attention our way. I have the safety of our whole community to consider. She must leave immediately." He pushes back his chair and stands up.

"With all due respect, sir," Jacob says, also rising to his feet, "my conscience would not allow me to send her back to the life she was leading."

"Then send her somewhere else," the Prophet says.

"Perhaps you could ask for the Divine's guidance," Jacob says quietly, "and assign her to a husband." He hesitates before continuing. "I would be honored to have a woman such as her as a wife."

A woman? A sister wife? I can't believe I'm hearing this.

The Prophet glares at him. "That would only make matters worse," he snarls. "You know exactly what they would say about us then. It's one thing to assign our own daughters to husbands, but something altogether different with a Gentile's daughter."

There is a silence in the kitchen. I can hear the floorboards creaking upstairs as the others get ready for bed.

"You have one week, Jacob, to find her a different place to live. She is no longer welcome in Unity or in The Movement."

He stomps out of the kitchen and slams the front door

behind him. Babies all over the house cry out as they are startled awake.

Jacob, Kelvin and I remain at the table in stunned silence. Eventually Kelvin speaks. "Nanette came to me last night, Taviana. She mentioned that Celeste is having impure thoughts and that you may be responsible for them."

I don't answer. I doubt his oldest daughter is the only girl in Unity having impure thoughts.

"Perhaps you have overstayed your welcome after all," he says. "I will help Jacob find a place for you to live in Springdale, or somewhere else, and we will try to find you work as well. I'll certainly vouch for your character and your work ethic."

I push my chair away from the table and stand up. "I never asked to come here," I tell the men. "Jacob invited me. I was surviving on my own before, and I will survive again. I don't need you to find me anything. A ride into Springdale tomorrow is all that I need."

"Taviana..." Jacob begins.

His eyes look so sad, and I think about how he offered to marry me to keep me here. "Thanks for all you've done, Jacob," I tell him. "This isn't your fault. You rescued me, and I've had a safe place to live for a year and a half. I have learned a lot. I appreciate that."

He looks like he's about to cry. It would do the Prophet good to take some sensitivity training from this man.

I leave the kitchen and begin to climb the back stairs to the upstairs bedrooms. Just as I reach the landing, I hear the back door creak open. I watch to see who could be coming in. A face peeks around the door, checking to see if the coast is clear. It's Celeste! Our eyes meet and I wave for her to go back outside.

Her eyes open wide, but she gets the message and steps back out the door. I continue up the stairs to the bedroom and climb into bed.

❊ Chapter Seven ❊

CELESTE

As soon as I poke my head in the house, I know that something has happened here tonight. It's like the air is electrically charged. It's late and everyone should be in bed, but Taviana's signal lets me know that someone must still be up. I step back outside and cross the yard to the barn. I hope Taviana will come and get me when it's safe to go in.

The minutes tick by. I crouch in the wet grass and lean against the barn wall. Looking up, I'm awed by the starry heavens. The moon is a slender crescent in the sky. I breathe deeply and let the stillness of the evening float gently down on me.

I should be worried. I should be remorseful. Instead I can't stop smiling. It feels exhilarating, being outside late at night, alone. I am not supposed to be here. I was not supposed to be at the river. A week ago I would have suffered agonizing guilt for such behavior, but today I'm only feeling a rush of joy at getting away with it. What has happened to me?

Eventually I see a figure slip out the side door of the house.

"Taviana, over here," I call out quietly.

Taviana makes her way over to where I'm crouching and takes my hand in hers. I can feel her shaking. Or is it me that's shaking?

"Let's go inside," I say, nodding toward the barn.

Sliding the door open, we slip through and inch our way down the corridor. Light from the moon shines through the broken slats in the walls and roof, but our eyes aren't yet accustomed to the dim light. We stumble upon a pile of old horse blankets that have been thrown into a corner. Taviana pulls me down onto them with her and we tug one over us to keep warm. I breathe in the musty scent of sweaty horse.

"Okay, you first," she tells me. "Where have you been?"

"I met Jon by the river." The words simply burst out of my mouth. So much for keeping it my little secret.

As soon as the words are out, I realize how inadequate my description of the evening is. I need to expand on it, explain how special it was, how scary, how sad and how exciting, but before I have a chance, she has her arms around me in a hug.

"Celeste! You monkey! I'd hoped that's what you were going to tell me, yet I didn't really believe you'd do it."

"You hoped?"

"Yeah, well, I know it's breaking rules and all that, but it's so clear you and Jon are hot for each other."

"Hot for each other?"

"Just an expression. So, spit it out. What happened?"

"Well." I sit back, remembering. "First we built rock statues."

"You what?"

I laugh at her question. "You remember that boy I told you about who made that amazing tower out of perfectly balanced rocks, the one that I destroyed?"

"The guy who cursed you with seven years' bad luck?"

"Right. Him." I smile at her in the darkness. So far the curse hasn't set in. "He also builds these rock...rock men. I saw him a few days ago, making one on the beach down by the playground, and after he left I made one beside his. Tonight I discovered he'd made a third one. Jon and I each made one more. Now there's a whole family of them."

"Inuksuk," Taviana says.

"Pardon?"

"Inuksuk. That's what those rock statues are called."

"They are? How do you know?"

"Just something I know about. Go on. What happened next?"

"Then...then we went and sat under the trees and talked."

"What did you talk about?"

"Just...stuff." Remembering the conversation quickly brings me down again, and I don't feel like sharing the details.

"C'mon, Celeste. You can do better than that."

"Well, he found an arrowhead on the beach and told me where it came from."

"And that's it?"

"No…he asked…he asked if I'd ever questioned the ways of The Movement."

"He did?"

"Uh-huh."

"And you said…"

"Yes."

"And then he said…"

"That he did too."

"And then?"

"He asked if I'd ever consider leaving Unity."

I could feel Taviana's body shift. "What did you say to that?"

"I said of course not! How could I?"

Taviana looks away, and I feel the arm that is pressed against mine become tense.

"What is it, Taviana?"

"Nothing. Tell me what else happened."

"Well…" Should I tell her? I decide I've come this far, I might as well go all the way, but my mouth goes dry.

"Well what?" she prompts.

"Then, well, then…"

"Celeste!"

"He kissed me."

Taviana pulls away so she can look directly into my face. "Are you serious?"

I nod and my heart swells at the memory of it.

"That is way cool!"

Way cool. Another of Taviana's odd sayings. "I don't know. It scared me. I ran off."

"You ran off?"

I feel my face burn as I nod. I decide to change the subject.

"So, now it's your turn," I tell her. "What happened here tonight?"

I can feel Taviana pull away from me, and suddenly I know something is terribly wrong. Here I am going on and on about my evening, and I haven't given one thought to what went on in hers.

"Celeste," Taviana says.

"Yeah?"

"I have bad news."

"What?" I feel my heart patter in my chest. "Is Mom okay? Rebecca?"

"They're fine."

"What then?"

"I'm leaving."

"Leaving?"

"Uh-huh. Tomorrow."

For a moment I don't understand what she's saying. "You're leaving Unity?"

She nods, and I see the shimmer of tears in her eyes.

"Why?"

"The Prophet ordered me to."

"He did? What happened?" I feel faint. How could

something so devastating have happened during the only two hours I've ever slipped away?

And then I know. This is all my fault. The surge of pleasure I'd experienced at being disobedient flips into total and utter remorse. This is God's way of punishing me.

"The police came," Taviana says. "They accused your family of keeping me—a runaway—here against my will. I was hiding in the crawl space, but after they left, the Prophet came over and told me I'd have to be gone within a week. He said he couldn't have the police snooping around here. I promised your father I would leave tomorrow."

"Oh no, Taviana, you can't."

"I have no choice, Celeste."

"This is all my fault!" I clutch onto her as sobs overwhelm me.

She holds me, and we rock together. Eventually she asks, "Why is this your fault?"

"Because I didn't practice purity. I was disobedient. I even enjoyed being disobedient. Now He's punishing me." I feel a wail coming on.

"You don't really believe that, do you, Celeste?" Taviana asks softly.

"Of course I do."

"Well I don't," she tells me firmly. "This has nothing to do with God. I'm just leaving because I make the Prophet nervous. Don't you dare think it has anything to do with you."

I wipe my nose with my sleeve. She's wrong, but I won't dwell on the point. "Where will you go?"

She shrugs. "It doesn't really matter. I've been homeless before. I'll survive."

"You won't…"

She squeezes my hand. "No, Celeste, I won't go back to that. I've been here too long." I can hear her swallow. "When I think about the me I was then…" She hesitates. "Well, I'm way different now."

"You liked living here?"

I see her nod in the dark. "Though I don't think I could have stayed here forever. I'm not one of you."

I nod. She's not.

"And I missed a few things."

"Like dishwashing machines."

"Yeah, and gum."

"Gum?"

"Yeah, and salt and vinegar chips. And books. And the Internet. Actually, a lot of things."

"So you're happy to leave." I don't know why that bothers me, but it does.

"No, this was a nice safe place to stay for a while, but it's time to move on."

I try to imagine the other kind of places she's been. I can't.

My eyes have become accustomed to the dark, and I see her smile. "In a sideways sort of way, Jacob offered to marry me tonight," she says.

"Really?"

"Yeah. It was so sweet. But the Prophet said no, and I wouldn't have consented to it anyway."

"Hmm." Consented. Have any of the girls from Unity ever consented to marriage? I decide to put that thought aside for later.

We sit in silence for a few minutes, leaning against each other. Her arm is warm on mine.

"Maybe you could ask Jon where the boys from Unity go when they leave," I suggest.

She doesn't say anything for a moment. Then she sits up. "Good call, Celeste. If I could get the name of someone, anyone, who'd take me in just long enough for me to... to get a job and save enough money to pay rent...then maybe..."

"Maybe what?"

Before she can respond, I'm startled by a voice calling my name. It's Daddy! We both jump to our feet.

"Let me do the talking," Taviana whispers.

I can only nod, too terrified to think of anything else. We step out the open door.

"Over here, Daddy."

He's standing by the back door, peering toward us. There's a smaller figure in a nightdress standing slightly behind him. Nanette. I should have known.

Taviana takes my hand and we approach.

"Where have you been?" he asks sharply.

"It's my fault," Taviana stammers. "I just wanted to tell Celeste what happened this evening."

"Weren't you here earlier?" he asks me.

I shake my head.

"Where were you?" he asks.

"I went for a walk," I say, but I can't look directly at him.

"A walk?" he asks. "Where to?"

"Just down to the river and back. It was such a nice evening, and all my chores were done."

"Were you alone?"

"Yes." Another lie. Something shrivels inside.

There's a long pause. I can feel him staring down at me. The agonizing guilt is reaching a breaking point.

"Could you not have waited until tomorrow to talk to Celeste, Taviana?" he asks. "Was this so urgent?"

"Yes, sir, it was urgent," Taviana tells him. "I'm leaving tomorrow, as you know. I wanted to spend some more time with her, to say good-bye. I may never see her again."

I feel my eyes well up again at the thought of that.

Father sighs and clears his throat. "Taviana, Nanette, get to bed. Celeste, you can come with me, into my office."

Taviana looks at me, alarmed. I can only shrug. Then I notice the smug look on Nanette's face, my little sister who I was so close to only a few short weeks ago. What has happened to us?

Taviana and Nanette go into the house, and I follow Daddy back into the barn. He flicks on the lights in his office and motions for me to take a chair.

"I was speaking with the Prophet this afternoon, Celeste," he says. "Before the…the unpleasant events of this evening."

My hand slides into the pocket of my apron and squeezes the arrowhead that Jon gave me. As I stroke its rough surface, I concentrate on seeing his face in my mind, his soft brown eyes. I will myself not to hear what my father is about to say.

"I urged him to hasten the announcement of your assignment," he continues, "as I understand you are being distracted by the boys in our community."

I clutch the pointed stone even tighter.

There's a long pause, and I can feel him studying me. "Is this true, Celeste?"

I swallow hard. I now know for sure that He is punishing me. First the news about Taviana, and now this. Do I dare tell another lie? "I just don't feel ready for marriage, Father. I would like to be something. Like a nurse, or a mechanic, like you."

His eyebrows arch.

"Or even a veterinarian," I continue. "I like being around farm animals."

He's staring at me like he's never seen me before.

"And," I add, almost under my breath, "I would like to choose my own husband."

I'm expecting an angry outburst, but Father simply leans back in his chair and folds his arms across his chest. "Your sister suggested Taviana might have been a bad influence on you. I didn't want to believe it, but I guess she was right. The sooner she leaves Unity, the better. It's a shame. She's been very helpful to your mother."

"Don't blame Taviana, Father." I can feel myself getting worked up. "You always said I asked too many questions. Now I'm asking myself whether I'm ready to be a good wife and mother, and the answer is no. Nanette is. Assign her to someone."

"You know it doesn't work that way," he says.

"Why can't I be the exception?"

"There are no exceptions, Celeste. You know that. We are all here for one reason, and that reason is to enter the Kingdom of Heaven together. If we make one exception, then we will have to make two, and so on. Taviana was an exception, and look how that turned out."

"It actually turned out fine. She's a good person."

"That may be so, but if she attracts attention to our little community, that is not a good thing."

"What will happen to her?"

"That's not for you to worry about."

"How can I not worry about her? I love her like a sister."

Father just shakes his head. "Why don't you concentrate on practicing purity? The greatest freedom we have is obedience. You're a good girl. You've been a fine daughter and a loving sister. I know you will also make a fine wife."

There's nothing for me to say. I concentrate on the stone again.

"I believe the Prophet will have a name for us within the next few weeks, Celeste, God willing. And then it will only be a few more weeks until the marriage will take place. I suggest you spend as much time as possible reading the scriptures. You will find the answers you seek there."

I get up to leave. "Good night, Celeste," he says.

"Good night."

I hear his chair squeak across the floor and then he mutters, "A veterinarian."

I glance back and see him shaking his head, a funny little smile on his face.

$\mathcal{N}anette$

I feel Celeste slide into bed, keeping to the far edge of the mattress. She turns her back to me. "I was worried about you," I whisper to her stiff back. "What if something had happened?"

"You weren't worried," she whispers into the dark room. "You were tattling. You want to get me into trouble."

I don't want to get her into trouble. I want to keep her *out* of trouble, but she won't believe that. "What did Father say?"

"He said that the Prophet's going to find me a husband as soon as possible because some little tattletale suggested I might be showing too much interest in boys my own age."

There's not much I can say to that, but I find myself smiling in the dark. Father listened to me. I wonder if he also asked the Prophet to assign me to a husband like I asked. Rolling onto my side, I snuggle under the blankets and sink back into the dream Celeste interrupted—the one where Martin Nielsson and I are standing facing each other, holding hands. "I've been waiting for this day for so long," he whispers, "and now here you are, finally, my wife." He leans forward, so close I can feel the heat radiating off his body. The next thing I know, his lips are on mine and our arms wrap around each other...

I WATCH AS Taviana pulls her suitcase out from under her cot and flips the lid open. The morning sun slants in through the window. Everyone but Taviana, Celeste and I has gone downstairs. Inside the suitcase are the clothes she arrived with. She pulls out a pair of blue jeans and a T-shirt. Celeste and I busy ourselves making beds while she gets dressed. When I hear the latch of the suitcase snap shut, I turn back to her. She's wearing pants that are skintight and sit low on her hips. The T-shirt appears to be two sizes too small, and there's a slash of skin exposed between the pants and the shirt.

"Taviana," I say, mortified for her. "I think you've outgrown those things."

She looks down at herself and shrugs. "No," she says, "they're right."

The outfit totally transforms her. She never quite fit in here, but now it's very clear that she's not one of us, never was. She looks completely unfeminine and unlikely to ever practice purity. Why would Gentile girls want to look like that? She hangs her nightdress in the closet beside her other dresses. They'll be passed down to one of our sisters or cousins.

Celeste is sitting beside the suitcase on the bed, tears streaming down her face. I feel a lump developing in my own throat. "How soon are you leaving?"

"Soon. Your father said to let him know when I'm ready. There are just a few people I want to go say good-bye to first." I notice the look that passes between her and Celeste, even through Celeste's tears.

"Like who?" I ask.

"Like..." She hesitates. "Like Jacob. He brought me here, and I lived with him and his family for the first six months." She glances at Celeste again.

A burning jealousy rips through me. When did Celeste and Taviana become so close? It's like Taviana has replaced me as Celeste's favorite sister.

"I'm going to ask Father if I can drive into town with you," Celeste tells Taviana.

Taviana shakes her head. "No," she says. "It will just make it harder. And besides, your mom needs you here."

Celeste doesn't argue but drops her face into her hands and her shoulders heave.

Settling onto the bed beside her, Taviana gently rubs her back. Then she says, "I'll be back in a few minutes." She gives Celeste's shoulders a last squeeze and walks out of the room. I follow her down the stairs.

Father usually goes directly to work after breakfast, but today he's still sitting at the kitchen table, across from Mother, who is not in bed for a change. His three other wives are present too, most of them with babies on their hips and toddlers hanging around their legs. Heads turn to stare when we walk into the kitchen and then just as quickly turn away. Taviana's lack of modesty is embarrassing. The mood remains somber, and even the children seem to sense that something is up. Mother is looking particularly weary.

"Are you ready, Taviana?" Daddy asks without looking at her.

"I need about fifteen minutes," she says. "To say good-bye."

"Most everyone's here," he says, looking around at his family. "Except the ones at school."

"There are a few others...like Jacob."

Father shakes his head. "I need to get going, Taviana. I have work to do."

"But..."

"And besides," he says, making a motion toward her with his hand, "you can't walk around Unity looking like that."

Red blotches appear on her cheeks. I wonder who she really wanted to say good-bye to.

"You can write some notes from the truck if you wish," Father says, "and I'll have one of the girls deliver them later."

I'm expecting her to put up a fight, but she places her suitcase on the floor with a sigh. "Then I'll just run up and say good-bye to Celeste," she says, dashing off before Father can respond. A few minutes later she's back. None of us have even moved. She picks up her suitcase, and with her shoulders thrown back, she turns and walks out the door.

We all gather around the truck. Father tosses Taviana's suitcase in the back and opens the passenger door for her, but instead of climbing in, she turns and looks into the faces of each of us standing there. My mother is not even trying to hold back her tears. They are streaming down her face. She's the first to embrace Taviana. "We're really going to miss you," she says.

"I'm going to miss you too," Taviana says, gently wiping the tears off Mother's face. "Thank you for taking me into your family."

I feel a tug in the pit of my stomach. Taviana has been taking care of Mother for weeks, helping her bathe, braiding her hair, keeping her company. Suddenly I realize that Taviana's developed a closeness with her that I've never had. I contribute to our home by helping with my little brothers and sisters, but I rarely get a chance to be alone with Mother. Right now I'm glad that Taviana's leaving. I will become Mother's caregiver. It's only right. I am her daughter.

Mother nods, clearly overcome, but unable to say anything else.

"And best of luck," Taviana says, gently rubbing Mother's swollen belly.

One by one, Taviana hugs each of the mothers, spending a little extra time with Pam, who is sobbing uncontrollably. Then she hugs many of the children. She takes Faith, one of the twins, and tosses her in the air. Faith squeals with delight. Taviana hugs her tightly before passing her back to Deborah. Joan, the other twin, raises her chubby arms up to Taviana. Taviana takes her from Lena and tosses her into the air too.

Finally she gets to me. We regard each other for a moment. "I'm really, really going to miss *you*, Nanette," she says.

"I'm really, really going to miss you too," I tell her, but I can no longer meet her eyes. I try to smile, but my mouth doesn't want to do what it's told. I feel it twist into what must be a ridiculous expression. Taviana wraps her arms around me and squeezes tight. "Be patient with Celeste," she whispers in my ear. "She's really a good person, just different from you."

I pull back to look at her. "You're good too," she says with a smile. "And the cheerful one."

I nod, remembering the pleasant times we spent together. When did all that stop? Things around here are shifting, and it makes me uneasy. It's a good thing she's leaving. Maybe things will go back to the way they were.

Dad clears his throat and Taviana climbs into the cab of the truck. She leans out the window and waves. Her eyes are shiny. We all wave back. I watch as they drive away, wondering if I'll ever see her again.

BACK IN THE house I settle Mother into bed, and then I gather up the twins and Rebecca. My brothers, Jerod and

Blake, are at school. I've decided not to go this morning. With Taviana gone, I'm needed here. I'll go back after the new baby is born.

Deborah is baking bread today, so I take her children into the living room too. I bring out a box of toys and settle down on the floor. Other children come in and out of the living room, and the morning ticks by in a steady rhythm. At noon I parade the children back into the kitchen and help the women serve them lunch. When I see that everything is under control, I take a tray of food up to Mother's room.

She's lying on her bed, her eyes open, and she smiles when she sees me. "Thanks, Nanette," she says. She reaches for a sandwich.

"Shall I say the blessing?" I ask.

She withdraws her hand and nods.

"For the food we are about to receive, may the Lord make us truly grateful."

"Amen." Pulling herself up, she again reaches for a sandwich. "With Taviana gone, I wondered if anyone would remember me."

"You thought I'd forget you?" I ask, hurt.

"I thought you'd be at school," she says and then frowns. "Where you're supposed to be."

"I'll go back to school after your baby is born," I tell her. "You need me now."

She studies me thoughtfully. "Maybe that's a good plan," she says. "It's not like you're learning anything there, is it?"

I shake my head. "I can either help at school or here, wherever I'm most needed. Right now I think I'm most needed here."

"I'll check with your father, but I appreciate the offer." She lays her hand on mine. It feels wonderful. We smile at each other.

"How are you feeling today?" I ask.

"Sad."

"Sad?"

"Yes, sad." She looks at me, puzzled. "Aren't you going to miss Taviana?"

"Oh that. Yeah." I try to sound sincere, but even I can hear the lack of enthusiasm in my response.

Mother sighs and pulls her hand away. "I've grown very fond of Taviana, and I ache inside when I think about what may become of her, alone in the world."

"But Mother, look at the way she was dressed today. She's not one of us."

She nods. "She was immodestly dressed by our standards, Nanette. But that's what she knows. It's how she was raised. With Taviana I learned to look beyond appearances to her character, and Taviana's is strong and resilient. There's a lot about her I admire."

"If she's so resilient, she'll be okay."

"I suppose, but there are so few options for girls out there."

I let that go. "What I really meant," I say, changing the subject, "is how are you feeling, you know, with the baby and everything?"

"Oh, about the same," she says. "Small cramps. I'm tired, but at least there's been no more bleeding."

"Bleeding?"

"Yes, bleeding. That's why I was put on bed rest."

"Oh."

"I think my poor body is telling me that there have been too many babies in too few years."

"Really?" I reach over to the tray and take a sandwich. This kind of talk makes me uncomfortable, but then I remember Taviana and my vow to become closer to my mother. "I thought it was the will of God for us to have many babies."

"That's true, Nanette," Mother says with a sigh, "but generally it's good to wait a year or two between them. Usually that happens when babies are on mother's milk, but I didn't seem to produce enough for the twins, so they had formula. That could be why I'm expecting again so soon."

"I can't wait to have my own babies," I tell her.

"Yes," she nods, though her eyes look sad. "Having a baby is a wonderful experience. Most of the time."

"I wish it was me and not Celeste that the Prophet is assigning to a husband."

"Oh dear," she sighs. "You've just reminded me that I'm soon to lose another daughter." She leans back and closes her eyes.

"Another daughter?"

"Taviana felt like a daughter."

"You'll still have me, for another year." Unless, of course, Father successfully convinces the Prophet to assign me to my own husband, but I don't mention this to Mother. She's feeling sad enough.

She doesn't open her eyes but says, "Thank goodness for that."

I reach over and take her hand in mine. This is the longest conversation I've had with her, just the two of us, for as long as I can remember. It hasn't been an especially happy talk, but having her all to myself is a sweet luxury.

"Nanette!" I hear my name being hollered from downstairs.

Sighing, I holler, "I'll be right there." I turn back to my mother. "Is there anything else I can get you?"

She shakes her head and I tuck the blankets around her, pick up the tray and retrace my steps down the stairs. In the kitchen I find my cousin, Sylvia, sitting in a chair. Our fathers are brothers, and Sylvia is my age, but we've never been close, maybe because Celeste has always been my closest friend. Until recently, anyway.

I take a closer look at Sylvia and see that her hair has come loose from its braid and is flying wildly around her face. Her eyes are wide and shiny, and she looks like she's in some kind of shock.

Deborah has pulled off her flour-covered apron and is stepping into outdoor shoes. She's frowning. "Colleen's in labor and there's some…" She glances at Sylvia. "Some… complications. I need to get over there. Nanette, you and Pam are to stay here with the children. Get them down for their naps. Celeste can…where *is* Celeste?" she asks, glancing around.

I haven't seen Celeste since Taviana's departure this morning. She often goes out to work in the garden, but I didn't see her come in for lunch. "I don't know."

Deborah sighs impatiently. "When you see her, tell her to…to make herself useful for a change."

I nod.

"And Lena can also help you when she gets back from the Coopers'. She's with her sister, who is also due soon. Her kids are there with her. When Kelvin gets back, tell him where I am."

Deborah steps out the door and looks back at Sylvia, still sitting mutely in the chair. "Do you want to stay here, honey?" she asks.

Sylvia shakes her head and seems to come out of her daze. She follows Deborah out the door. Through the window I see them practically running down the road to the rambling house where Colleen, the youngest wife of Uncle Jeremy, lives. She's seventeen, and this is her first baby.

Pam and I round up the children, and one by one we get them into their cribs and settled. Back in the kitchen, I finish cleaning up from lunch, and Pam gets busy with laundry.

I'm sweeping the floor, wondering what "complications" could possibly mean, when I see the truck pull up to the side of the house. When Daddy comes in, he looks around. "Where's Deborah and Lena?"

"At Uncle Jeremy's house. Colleen's having her baby, and there are complications."

"What kind of complications?"

I just shrug.

He turns and starts back out the door. "Daddy?"

He wheels around to stare at me. "Yes?"

"Celeste has been missing all morning."

"Missing?"

"She hasn't been here. No one seems to know where she is."

He studies me for a moment and then hurries back out, and I see him jogging down the street toward his brother's house.

I feel a tug of guilt, knowing I just tattled again, but I'm really getting concerned about her. This disappearing act can only be bad news, and there was something about the way Taviana and Celeste were looking at each other this morning that increased my suspicions.

When the kitchen is tidy, I join Pam in the backyard and help her hang diapers on the line. She's not much older than Celeste and is the quietest girl I've ever met. We've been waiting almost a year for her to announce that she's with child, but so far that hasn't happened. She's looking particularly pale this afternoon. For some reason she was especially attached to Taviana, despite how different they were, and she always gets anxious when there's any kind of conflict in our home.

Just as we're finishing up the diapers, I see Celeste coming through the gate behind the garden. She waves and carries on toward the house.

"Where have you been?" I call out to her.

"In the garden," she says, without stopping.

Does she really think I'll believe her? I would have seen her if she'd been in the garden. "Father's looking for you," I tell her.

Now she does stop and swings about to face me. "What did you tell him?"

"That you haven't been seen all morning or for lunch."

"Thanks, Nanette," she says. "You're such a big help."

I don't get a chance to respond because Father's suddenly running into the side yard and jumping into his truck. He begins to back out of the driveway.

I race over, and he rolls down his window. "I'm going back to town to get a doctor," he says.

"Is she okay?"

"I don't know. It doesn't look good."

I watch as he drives away. The warm day suddenly feels chilly. *It doesn't look good.* What could have happened? She was looking so beautiful in church just last Sunday. I'd stared at her, fascinated. From the back she looked exactly as she did nine months ago, tiny and slim, her golden braid hanging to her waist, but when she turned you could see her protruding belly. The baby was almost due, and I tried to imagine it folded up inside her, all the little fingers and toes wiggling, the wispy hair, the button nose. How I longed to be with child myself.

But now things don't look good. That changes everything.

I'm lifting Faith out of her crib and carrying her to the diaper change table when I hear a siren. Looking out the window, I see the ambulance screaming down the road. Pam, who was in the kitchen, races out the front door and directs the driver to the correct house.

The afternoon drags by. Father has returned, parked his truck in the driveway and returned to his brother's house. Celeste is in the kitchen, preparing the evening meal. Pam and I are taking care of the children. School is out, and with no one available to take them to the playground, the older children are racing around the house and yard. I usually enjoy their high spirits, but today I'm irritable and wish they'd all go away.

Just when I don't think I can take it anymore, Celeste calls me into the kitchen. "Look," she says. "The ambulance is leaving."

We watch as it drives past our front yard. This time there are no flashing lights or sirens. We continue watching out the window and soon see Daddy and Deborah coming down the road. Deborah is clutching Daddy's hand and leaning on him.

Celeste and I are still standing, frozen to the spot, when the two of them come in the front door. I meet Deborah's eyes. She just shakes her head, sadly.

"What happened?" I find myself crumpling into a chair. "She was so healthy, so beautiful."

"Sometimes God takes the beautiful ones early," Deborah says. She sinks into a chair beside mine. Her face is pale and her eyes bloodshot.

"But, but what happened?"

"It seems that something tore inside her," Deborah

explains. "It caused heavy bleeding. We couldn't make it stop."

I think about Mother and how she said she too had been bleeding, but I'm afraid to ask if it could be the same thing.

"Was she in pain?" Celeste asks, crying quietly. Lena and Pam have joined us at the table.

"No, not at all," Deborah assures her. "She never even went into labor." We sit in stunned silence for a few more minutes. Then Deborah adds, "The doctor who came with the ambulance was able to save the baby, through surgery, but it was too late for Colleen." She rubs her face. "It's a girl."

"What if the doctor had been here sooner?" Celeste asks.

Deborah shoots her a scathing look but doesn't answer.

"I'm going upstairs to break the sad news to Irene," Daddy says, rising from his chair. He looks across the table to Celeste. "And I'll talk to you later."

As soon as Daddy has left the room, Deborah turns to Celeste. "You are right out of line asking questions like that," she scolds. "It was in God's hands. How horrid of you to make your father feel worse than he already does." Her chair scrapes away from the table, and she briskly scoops up Colin, her son, who has been tugging on her dress. She stomps out of the kitchen.

Celeste and I glance at each other. Is she wondering about Mother too? She shrugs and returns to the sink, where she's peeling potatoes. I notice the firm set of her jaw.

I gather up the twins and return to the big room, but I can't find the energy to amuse them. I lie on the floor, and they crawl and totter around me. I think about Colleen, only seventeen and gone. How will her family cope with this tragedy? I know she is with God now, in Heaven, but it is still so sad. I watch as Faith pulls herself up on the coffee table and leans toward a toy on the other side. Not able to reach it, she inches her way around the table, step by step. Colleen will never see her baby take her first steps. Or say her first words.

A fresh wave of sadness washes over me. I feel the need to be with someone, to share the sadness. I consider going back to the kitchen to be with Celeste, but then I remember the coolness that has come between us. And Daddy is with Mother.

Rebecca, who has been piling blocks into a tower, suddenly stops what she's doing and comes to sit beside me.

"Are you sad, 'Net?" she asks.

I nod and look down at her.

"Me too," she says quietly and pops a thumb into her mouth.

"How come you're sad?" I ask her. I doubt she even knew who Colleen was.

"I miss Taviana."

I nod. This makes sense. She would have been part of the good-bye crowd this morning. All the children loved her.

Taviana. Where is she right now? And where will she sleep tonight? I pull Rebecca into my lap and hug her to me.

"I miss her too," I say, and I realize, despite myself, that it's true.

We sit quietly, watching the babies explore the living room and listening to the sniffling coming from the women in the kitchen.

Chapter Nine

CELESTE

M y hands are wet and dirty with potato peeling, so I use the sleeve of my dress to wipe my nose. Colleen has died. Sweet pretty Colleen. Why would God take someone so pure instead of a horrible disobedient person like me? I rinse my hands and dry them on a dishtowel, and then I reach into my pocket and pull out the hanky I find there. With a shock I discover it's Jon's. I shove it back in and a fresh wave of remorse floods over me as I remember how I spent the day while Colleen fought for her life, and lost.

I HADN'T MOVED off my bed until I heard the crunch of tires on the driveway this morning. I couldn't believe Daddy was actually taking Taviana away. How could he do that to someone who had given so much of herself to our family?

The sadness that had weighed me down all night changed into a burning anger. Jacob should never have brought Taviana to our community if we weren't able to keep her. The Prophet should have spoken up a year and a half ago, before we'd taken her in, before we began loving her. And Daddy. How could he simply drive a family member into town and dump her there, like a stray cat, knowing that, unlike a cat, she couldn't possibly make it on her own?

In the bathroom, I washed my face with cold water and rebraided my hair. I straightened my shoulders, walked out of the bathroom and descended the stairs as calmly as I could.

Daddy's wives were each busy with chores so no one paid any attention to me. I picked up a basket of soggy laundry and pushed my way through the door. Leaving the basket on the step, I headed toward the garden and carried right on out through the back gate.

There was one last thing I could do for Taviana. She'd hoped to talk to Jon herself, but Daddy didn't allow her any time so I was going to do it for her. I told her I'd do it, and I wouldn't let her down.

I reached the road and found it deserted. As I passed the Nielsson compound, I saw Jon pounding nails into fencing just outside the barn. Relief flooded through me. I don't know what I would have done if he hadn't been there. I only glanced at him briefly, but our eyes met and I knew he'd see me heading toward the river, alone. I hoped he understood what that meant.

Slipping into the shadowy hidden area that we'd sat in just the night before, I crouched down and leaned back against a tree. I thought it might take a while before Jon could slip away from his work to join me, but I didn't care. I had to pass on the message.

From my hiding place, I had a partial view of the inuksuk, as Taviana called them. Seeing them helped calm me. The erect statues continued to stand guard, watching the river flow past. I wondered what the boy would think when he saw the two new additions to the family. I smiled, just thinking of what my reaction would have been. If we kept this up, the entire river would someday be watched over by these rock men.

I sensed Jon's presence before I saw him. He was standing behind me, looking down. "What are you smiling about?" he asked.

"Oh, just those statues." I shook my head and waved in their direction, embarrassed at being caught this way. "There's…there's just something about them that pleases me."

Jon nodded. "I know what you mean." He offered me a hand and pulled me to my feet. When I was up, he continued to hold my hand, but I pulled it away, nervous. We didn't have the protection of dusk to hide us today.

"I didn't expect to see you again so soon," he said, ignoring my gesture.

"No, I guess you didn't." I tried to smile but it felt awkward. The comfort level we'd achieved between us the night before had evaporated, and I was suddenly shy. I decided to get right to the reason for my being there.

"Jon…"

"Yes?" He tipped his head and looked hard at me.

"Taviana is gone."

"Gone?"

"Yes. The Prophet ordered her out of Unity," I told him.

"Why?"

"Apparently the police came looking for her last night, when we were here." I blushed, thinking of how the evening had ended. "He thinks that she draws unwelcome attention to our community."

"It's taken him until now to decide that?"

I could only shrug.

"So what will happen to her?"

I sighed. "Father drove her to Springdale this morning. He's just going to leave her there, to fend for herself." My voice was shaky, and then I felt my eyes filling with tears again. I covered my face with my hands, hoping to make them go away, but the next thing I knew, Jon had his arms around me and I melted into him, sobbing into his shoulder. He held me tight. When the tears were finally finished and my ragged breathing had returned to normal, we continued standing there, wrapped in each other's arms, rocking gently from side to side. The pain had subsided, for the moment. I finally dragged myself away from him and wiped my cheeks. "Sorry about that," I said.

"Don't be sorry." He pulled a handkerchief out of his back pocket and handed it to me. "It's clean," he said, smiling.

I scrubbed at my cheeks again and blew my nose. "Not anymore," I told him. I shoved it into a pocket of my apron. "I'll return it after it's been washed."

"So…" he asked. "What are we going to do about Taviana?"

His question startled me. What are *we* going to do? Not only did he understand that something had to be done, but he was offering to help me. I lunged forward and hugged him, hard, all shyness gone.

"Whoa!" he said as I released him. "What was that for?"

"For saying just the right thing."

"What did I say?"

"You offered to help do something for Taviana."

"Oh, that's it? If I say it again…"

"No." I punched him lightly on the arm. He laughed.

"Taviana wanted to come and talk to you herself this morning," I told him, "but she wasn't given any time. She says you know people in Springdale who might be able to help her."

Jon nodded. "I know some guys who have left Unity. I don't know exactly what they could do for her, but…"

"I just keep picturing her sleeping…I don't know where. Under a tree? In a doorway?"

"No, we can't let that happen." He thought for a moment. "The problem is I don't know when the guys will be coming by for another visit. It could be tonight or it could be two weeks from now."

"Two weeks?"

Jon frowned. "I do have a telephone number for Jimmy. He gave it to me for the time when…" He didn't finish the sentence, but I knew what he was going to say. For the time when he left Unity.

"But what good is a number without a telephone?"

"I could walk to the highway and hitchhike to the nearest house and knock on doors until I find someone who will let me use their phone."

"When would you do this?"

"Today." He looked surprised that I'd asked. "A little later. Jimmy will be at work right now."

"But won't you get into trouble?"

He shrugged. "I can live with the consequences."

"What will those consequences be?" I didn't want him to get punished for helping me.

"Don't worry about it, Celeste," he said quietly. "Like I said last night, I'm not happy in Unity anyway. The best thing they could do is kick me out of the house."

I looked away so he couldn't see how I felt about that, but he must have figured it out anyway. "I really think you should consider your options too," he said.

"I told you last night. I don't have any options."

"I think you should think harder about that."

I shook my head.

We stood quietly for a moment. I knew I should go home, but I couldn't drag myself away. Who knew when I'd see him again.

Eventually Jon reached out and took my hand. He clasped it in both of his. Then he looked directly into my face.

"You look so sad, Celeste. Why don't we build a couple more statue people, just for fun."

"Someone might see us."

"No one comes down here."

"But what if…"

He put a finger to my lips. "Shh. This is your life, Celeste. Sometimes you can do things just for you. Just for fun."

"But…"

"No buts. C'mon." He dragged me toward the statues. I resisted, but he was stronger and I found myself stumbling along behind him. I glanced over my shoulder, back toward the community, but a row of trees hid the beach from the road. By the time we reached the statues I was laughing. He laughed too.

"I'm going to make a lady statue this time," I told him.

He nodded. "Good idea. These guys could use a wife or two."

"Are you kidding? This wife is going to have a whole bunch of husbands."

Jon laughed so hard he had to wipe tears from his eyes. "Now you're thinking outside the box."

"Outside the box?"

He smiled. "It's a saying I heard once. It means thinking creatively."

"Oh." Outside the box. I liked that. I would use it on Taviana and surprise her. And then I remembered Taviana was gone. There would be no more stories, no more funny expressions.

"So, how are you going to make this lady, the one who has many husbands?" Jon asked.

"You just watch."

He let go of my hand and I began combing the beach, looking for a large, triangle-shaped rock. I looked back and saw that Jon had already found two blocky stones for legs. I kept searching. Eventually I saw exactly what I needed, but when I tried to pick it up, I realized it was way too heavy for me to carry alone. "Will you give me a hand?" I called.

He came over, and together we lifted the rock, but when we tried to carry it across the beach, I found that I was tripping over my dress. "I guess I'll have to make her right here," I told him, placing my end down.

"Why?"

"My dress…it gets in the way. I'll end up ripping it."

"Think outside the box, Celeste."

"Huh?"

"Like you did the other day, when I was watching you."

I felt my face burn. "How long were you watching?"

"Long enough."

It was one thing for him to have seen my legs from a long distance away, but quite another for me to hitch my dress up right there in front of him. "No, I can't do that."

"I won't look, I promise."

I laughed at his silly remark.

"Okay then," he said, "I'll only look at you from the waist up."

"You're embarrassing me."

"Oh, c'mon, Celeste. They're just ankles, and maybe knees. What's so private about that?"

I thought about it. He was right. It was really only my ankles that would show. Before I could change my mind I bent over, grabbed my hem and tucked it into the sash of my apron. I glanced at Jon. He was staring at my saggy-stocking-covered ankles. I smacked his arm. "You said you wouldn't look!"

"I lied," he said, grinning. Then he bent over and lifted his side of the large stone. I just shook my head, picked up my side, and together we carried it over to where the family of statues was waiting.

"Thanks," I said, and I tipped the stone so that one of the corners pointed to the sky. I then balanced another rock on the point. It took a moment to find the right angle and make it secure, but I did. The arms, neck and head followed. I stepped back to admire my creation. She was perfect. The triangular stone looked just like a skirt.

I looked toward Jon. He was standing there, watching me. I quickly pulled my dress back down and straightened it. When I looked up again, he was smiling. "Now that wasn't so terrible, was it?" he asked.

I just shook my head, smiling. Together we moved back on the beach so we could view the whole scene from a distance. The boy would be very surprised when he next visited this part of the beach.

Jon took my hand and we walked back to the sheltered area under the trees. "Will you think about what I said, Celeste?" he asked.

"About thinking out of the box?"

"Exactly. Consider your options."

I nodded. "Okay."

Then I let Jon kiss me. I even kissed him back, surprised at how natural it felt. Our arms were around each other, and as his soft lips explored mine, my worries slipped completely away. I was only aware of the intense sensations that were swirling inside me. It wasn't until my stomach growled that I realized how much time had passed.

"I better go," I said, breaking off the kiss, but still holding him close.

"Yeah, me too," he said. He stepped back so he was looking down at me. "One way or another, I'll make that phone call today. I know Jimmy will do whatever he can to help. He knows a lot of people."

"Thanks, Jon."

His lips brushed mine once more, and then I left him and headed toward the road. He'd follow a few minutes later.

My mind whirled all the way home, and I felt... different. I hadn't known how good a kiss could feel. I would have skipped home if it wouldn't have drawn unwanted attention my way.

And then I heard the news, the news about Colleen, and my world came crashing down.

Daddy, who has been upstairs comforting Mother, calls me from the doorway. "Celeste, I want to see you in the barn."

When we were small children, those dreaded words would have meant we were in for a whipping, but once Nanette and I reached age twelve, Daddy quit reaching for the whip and just talked to us. I nod and follow him across the side yard.

Sitting across the desk from him, I notice the dark smudges under his eyes. Sometimes I wonder how he manages to lord over so many people. Do any of the men of The Movement ever wish they had fewer wives and children? I shake my head and push the thought away. That would be against the principles that the Prophet has laid out. Our men know they need at least three wives before they can enter the Kingdom of Heaven. More than three is preferred.

"Where were you this morning, Celeste?" Daddy asks me, his voice weary.

I close my eyes to relieve the burning sensation. There has been so much crying today. First Taviana. Then Colleen. Should I do the right thing and tell him the truth? I open my eyes and swallow hard. "I was feeling so sad about Taviana leaving that I…" I haven't told the lie yet. I can still do the right thing. I don't. "I went for a walk to clear my head."

"To clear your head?"

"Yes."

"Celeste, do I need to remind you that with your mother in bed you are needed at home more than ever?"

Perhaps I am possessed by the devil. I simply don't know why I say some of the things that I do. The words just blurt out of my mouth. "If that's the case, Father, then I don't think this would be a good time for me to be married."

I have closed my burning eyes again, but I can feel him staring at me. A full minute passes before he replies. "If it weren't for your age, Celeste," he says finally, "I'd take the strap off the wall and whip that contrariness right out of you."

I don't comment, but I open my eyes and stare at my feet.

"I just hope that whoever you are assigned to does a better job with you than I have."

"I just hope that I don't die in childbirth at seventeen years old."

Father sighs. "It is not for us to question the ways of the Lord," he says.

"Are we finished here?" I ask him. "I need to get back to preparing dinner."

"Not quite. First of all, I want you to know that I didn't intend to simply push Taviana out the door of the truck and leave her in Springdale, on her own. I planned to speak to people I knew, to see if I could help find her some work." He shakes his head. "But she wouldn't let me. I suggested we go to the church. They would find shelter for her, but again, she refused my offer of help."

Taviana and her pride. Why couldn't she have swallowed it just this once?

"We don't have much money, as you know, Celeste, but I was able to get her to take one hundred dollars, to tide her over until she finds work. It was a gift, but she insists that she'll repay it."

"I'm sure she will."

"She won't go hungry for a few days anyway."

I nod. If he's expecting me to applaud him for his generosity, he's mistaken.

"Promise me there will be no more disappearing," he says.

"Promise me I won't be assigned to a husband," I respond.

He glares at me as he gets to his feet. "It's been a long day, Celeste. Your disrespect is not appreciated."

He's right about that. It has been an incredibly long day, and there are an endless number of chores yet to be done. I follow him across the yard to the house.

Chapter Ten

Taviana

It's as though the time I spent in Unity never even happened. I'm standing on a sidewalk, alone, with one hundred dollars in my pocket. I have nowhere to go, nothing to do. Did I just dream the past eighteen months into existence?

One part of me, the part that felt at home in Unity, tells me to get on with it, find a place to live and some kind of work. The other part of me, the part that's longing for a little excitement, wants me to ditch my suitcase in a locker at the bus station and explore the town. After very little soul-searching, that's the part of me that wins out.

I wander the streets looking for...I'm not sure what. The usual businesses are all here, the services, the community center. The kids are in school. There's really not much to explore after all, and I quickly grow bored. It's a familiar sensation, this lack of purpose. It's the way I lived for years. I notice how easy it is to leave behind the girl I was in

Unity and slip back into my old self. An uneasiness gnaws at my stomach. How long before I slide right back to my old lifestyle, the me I was before I moved to Unity? When I lived there, I temporarily became someone different, someone in a long dress, an apron and practical shoes. That girl learned to fit into her new community, to be good and obedient. Is there no way to blend the two me's?

I round a corner and stumble upon the library. A smile bubbles up from deep inside. It's like running into an old friend. I've spent countless hours in libraries, keeping warm, using the washroom, reading, surfing the net. That was the best part, being able to escape my life and enter an entirely new one for a few hours.

The librarian smiles at me when I push open the door. I smile back and savor the dusty smell of old books. The New Arrivals display is right by the entrance. One of the book covers is intriguing, and I pick it up and read the description on the back flap. *A story of romance, of regret, of redemption. This is the gripping tale of a woman haunted by her past.* Except for the romance part, this could be my life. I think of Celeste, how she loves stories and how I wish I could see her set loose in a library. It would truly be heaven on earth for her. But that's not going to happen.

Taking the book with me, I head over to the racks of DVDs and scan the titles. This would really boggle Celeste's mind. There is no end of stories. I continue wandering through the library until I come to a bank of computers and plunk myself down at an available one.

An hour passes before I drag my eyes away from the screen. I've just brought myself up to date on what has happened in the world in the past couple of years. It still boggles my mind that the people in Unity are completely unaware of what is going on out here. Maybe that's a good thing. Most of the news is dreary, and there's nothing anyone can do about it anyway.

I'm approaching the checkout with my book when I remember that I can't borrow it. The kind librarian reads my face. "Do you need to apply for a card?" she asks.

I nod, and she slides a sheet of paper across the counter to me. "Just fill out this application form and return it with some identification that includes your address."

That settles it. I have no address, no phone number and no identification. I used to be able to use my mother's, but that was another town. I guess I won't be getting a library card.

"I'll bring it back tomorrow," I tell her, placing the novel back on the shelf. I shove the form in my pocket and head out the door, empty-handed, feeling like I've just been turned away from the soup kitchen.

The soup kitchen. My stomach growls and I remember passing a row of fast-food restaurants just around the corner. Fast food. My mouth waters at the thought of biting into a burger oozing with tangy sauce. I retrace my steps, passing places that offer fried chicken, tacos and submarine sandwiches. They all sound good, but I know what I want for my first meal back in the real world. I order a cheese and bacon burger, French fries and a Coke. Extra large.

Unwrapping the burger from the paper, I lick the excess relish off it, savoring the experience. The first bite is so good I hardly swallow before I'm taking the second one. Then I shovel in a handful of salty French fries and slurp down a mouthful of Coke. This is a complete and welcome change from all those wholesome meals I ate in Unity. I repeat the process but force myself to slow down.

When the burger is half gone, my stomach suddenly retaliates. It bloats and gurgles. I gaze at the remaining food. The paper that the hamburger was wrapped in is saturated with grease, as is the container half full of fries. Now my stomach lurches. Getting up, I throw the rest of the food in the garbage and race to the bathroom.

Half an hour later, when the cramps have passed, I'm again wandering around town. I find myself at a park and figure that this is where kids my age will gather at the end of their school day. I should be able to hook up with some of them then.

I cut across the grass and down the bank to the river. The day is getting warm and I decide to wade barefoot in the water, something that is taboo for girls in Unity, who even swim in their long dresses. Crossing the rocky beach, I spot a cluster of rock shapes farther down the river. Remembering Celeste's experience here, I wander over to take a look.

As I get closer, I'm stunned by what I see and now understand why Celeste had to check to see if the stones were glued together. The towers really do appear to defy gravity, they balance so precariously. Large stones, point down, perch on smaller stones, which in turn are carefully balanced on the stones beneath them. Each one is a small miracle. I circle around them and wonder why their creator would build these unique works of art here, where anyone could knock them over.

I decide that this is as good a place as any to wade into the river. Squatting down, I pull off my shoes and socks and roll up my jeans. The stones are sharp under my feet, but I hobble across the beach and wade into the water. It is ice-cold, and all my senses snap to attention. I wade out to where a boulder juts out of the water and scramble onto it.

The sun is warm, and I stretch out across the flat top of the huge rock. The heat on my skin and the soothing sound of the rushing water makes me sleepy. I lie back and close my eyes.

Sometime later I wake from my nap. Sitting up, I look around and discover I am no longer alone. The rock balancer is back on the job.

I sit as still as I can and watch him. He must know I'm here—my shoes and socks are heaped in the center of his circle of balanced rocks—but he's in total concentration. His current project already has two base rocks, one balancing on the other. Now he is cradling a third one in his hands. His feet are spread apart and his knees are bent, as if he too is balanced. He gently touches the new rock to the structure but does not appear to loosen his grip on it. Ever so slightly he moves the rock around the thin tip of the one he is placing it on. He is totally focused on the task, and if I didn't know better, I'd say he was hypnotized by it. Five, ten minutes pass. He is still trying to find the point of balance for his new rock. Now I see him slowly letting go of the rock. It stays. He straightens up and takes a step back. A new rock balance has been created. I feel like I've just seen a performance, and I begin to clap wildly. He appears to wake out of a trance as his head snaps around to look at me. For a brief moment I'm afraid he'll be mad that I was watching, that this was a private moment for him, but then his face breaks into a goofy grin and he bows.

I climb off my boulder and wade back through the water to the beach. "That's amazing!" I say as I stumble toward him. "I can't believe I saw you balance that rock there. I would have sworn it was impossible."

"Anything is possible," he tells me, still grinning.

"So why do you do this, this rock-balancing thing?" I ask him. I've plunked myself down on the beach to pull on my socks and shoes.

"Because I enjoy it," he says. He's still smiling.

"That's it? Just because you like it?"

"What other reason do I need?"

There's something really appealing about this guy. He seems so naturally serene. I suspect he goes around with a smile on his face all the time. "I dunno. Maybe because it brings you peace or it's a spiritual experience or it's how you worship Mother Nature."

"Yep, it's all of those things too. It's whatever you want it to be."

"Hmm." I admire the formations for a few moments. "A friend of mine said she was here, and she accidentally toppled one over."

He tilts his head and frowns. "Was that the girl with the long skirt? From Unity?"

"Yeah, that was her."

"I felt terrible, scaring her off like that. I wanted to talk to her."

"No chance of that. Girls from there aren't permitted to talk to guys like you."

"Guys like me?"

"Guys period. But especially with guys who aren't from The Movement."

"That's a shame. There was something very...very sweet about her."

"Innocent. They are completely sheltered from the real world."

"How do you know this girl?"

"I lived with her family for over a year."

"But you're not one of them?"

"Hey! How can you tell?" I look down at my T-shirt and jeans and then back at him. "Don't I look sweet and innocent?"

"Yeah, but..." he blushes.

"Okay, you're right." I smile and let him off the hook. "But they took me in for a while and helped me get out of a bad space I was in. Now they've kicked me out, but that's okay. I'm a better person for it."

"Why'd they kick you out?" He has joined me, sitting on the beach. I see that his hands are busy stacking pebbles, one on top of the other.

"The Prophet decided I was a danger to their way of life. It's okay, I'm not one of them and never would be."

"This girl, the one I met on the beach, do you think she could be the one who is building inuksuks in Unity?"

"Yeah, I know she is."

He gets a funny look on his face. "Then I have been communicating with her, just not in words."

I study his profile. His features are fine, almost chiseled. He wears his black hair long and tucks it behind his ears. He's exotic looking, and I wonder what his family background is. "What's your name?" I ask.

"Craig. And you are?"

"Taviana." I shake his outstretched hand.

"What's your friend's name?" he asks.

"Celeste." I glance at him. Why does she attract all the cute ones? "But don't go getting any ideas. She's getting married soon."

"Married?"

"Yep. They marry their girls young."

"How does Celeste feel about that?"

"She's not happy, but there's not a lot she can do about it."

"Why not?"

"It's just the way they do things. And she can't leave, she'd have nowhere to go. She doesn't have much education, and she's not trained for any kind of work." I consider what I've just said. "She'd be in the same predicament that I'm in."

"Which is?"

"Nowhere to live, no education, no job."

"That's not good." Craig frowns.

The difference, I think to myself, is that I know how to survive on the streets. Celeste wouldn't have a chance. I decide to change the subject. "So, how come you're not in school?"

"I graduated last year, on the coast. My parents wanted to shake their lives up a bit, so my dad took a job here and I moved with them." He pauses. "I haven't decided what to do with my life yet, so I mostly just help my dad out. And balance rocks." He smiles.

"And build inuksuks," I remind him.

"Right. Those too."

"What does your dad do?"

"He's a vet, specializing in farm animals. That's why I'm often in Unity. I go with him on his rounds to all the rural communities, but when I get tired of listening to him talk to the farmers about the weather or which bull calves will be castrated, I look for a place where I can build something with rocks."

"Celeste has dreams of being a vet."

"She does?"

"Uh-huh. Poor thing. She'll have half a dozen kids by the time she's old enough to go to university. And with only a grade-eight education, and no support from her parents or husband..." I shake my head. "She hasn't got a hope."

Craig is silent, studying his rock art. Then he says quietly, "Someone should tell her that anything is possible. Check out the rocks."

We both study them for a moment. "Not for a girl from Unity."

"Then that's sad." I watch as Craig uses his finger to topple one of his mini-rock balances.

"Don't your parents expect you to go to school or work or something?"

He nods. "But I can't figure out what it is I want to do. There's no point spending the money on school if I don't know what to take."

I nod.

"And I haven't searched too hard for a job," he admits.

We sit quietly, pondering our lives. "What happened to your real family?" he asks softly.

"I never knew my dad," I tell him. "I don't even know if my mom knew who he was. And I didn't get along with my mom, so I ran away when I was twelve. I've been on my own ever since."

"Wow," he says. "I'm impressed."

"Don't be," I tell him. "I haven't done anything I'm terribly proud of."

"Not yet," he says. "But you must be a survivor. That counts for something."

I shrug. "Who knows."

"So where are you living?"

"Nowhere yet. I just arrived today, but I'm pretty sure that I have a connection that is going to help me out." I make it sound like it is more of a sure thing than it is. I don't need his pity right now.

Something jangles in his pocket. He pulls out his cell phone and checks the screen before pushing it back into his pocket. "I have to go," he says, "but I hope I see you around."

"Yeah," I say, climbing to my feet too. "I hope so."

I watch as Craig disappears into the forest directly behind us. I head back toward the park.

THE AFTER-SCHOOL crowd has arrived, just as I'd expected it to. I study the scene from my shadowy hiding place at the edge of the park, trying to determine which group of kids appears most approachable. The various ages have staked out their own picnic tables and are lounging on them, pretending not to notice the kids at other tables. A few boys kick a soccer ball back and forth, and hacky sacks are being kept in the air by nimble feet. Two of the tables appear to be designated smoking areas and attract kids of all ages.

I finally decide that boys won't see me as a threat, so I approach an all-male table of senior-looking guys.

Someone at the table must have noticed me walking across the park toward them and then said something to the others, because all their heads swing to look in my direction.

"Hi," I say as casually as I can when I arrive at their table.

"Hey." A few nod politely, and curious expressions cross some of the boys' faces.

"New here?" a skinny guy asks. I notice the tattoos that run up both his forearms. They might be antlers, but I'm not sure.

"Yeah. Just arrived today."

"Where from?" he asks.

I hesitate, not sure whether to tell the truth, but because I can't come up with a lie fast enough, I let it spill. "Unity."

That gets a reaction. They all study me a little harder.

"You don't look like someone from Rabbitsville," a small stocky guy sneers.

I sense some uncomfortable squirming from the other boys.

"Rabbitsville?"

"That's what some people call Unity," the guy with the tattoos explains. I notice he's blushing slightly.

"That's kind of random," I say, faking innocence although I have a pretty good idea what it refers to.

"It's because of all the babies that are born there," the stocky boy says, looking directly at me. It's a challenge, a test. I feel the embarrassed glances of the other boys too, waiting for my reaction. "As in," he continues, "rabbits are known for making lots of bunnies."

I just shrug. "I found it weird at first too, all those babies, and the sister wives, but I was only a visitor for a year and a half, so I'm not really from there."

"Why would you visit a place like that?" a third boy asks. He climbs off the table and stretches, and I notice the long ripple of muscle in his bare arms.

"Long story," I tell him. "But I won't be going back."

The boys seem to relax, and I decide I've passed the test.

Their attention suddenly shifts to another girl who is crossing the park, coming toward us. She has a cell phone

SISTER WIFE

clamped to her ear, and she's wearing a mini-skirt and high wedged heels. She takes long purposeful strides on chopstick-thin legs. Her T-shirt is scooped low and her melon-sized breasts remain surprisingly still, even though her thick blond ponytail swings wildly from side to side. I can't help but think how much she looks like some of the girls I used to work with. When she arrives she gives me a quick once-over, clamps her phone shut and plants herself in front of the boy with the muscles. Their lips lock and the rest of us look away.

"So," I say, "anyone know where I might find some work in this town?"

"You don't go to school?" tattoo-guy asks.

I shake my head.

"What kind of work are you looking for?"

"The kind that pays money."

"I haven't seen any help-wanted signs for a while," he says, shrugging.

"Who are you anyway?" the girl asks. She's unglued herself from muscle-boy and is eyeing me suspiciously.

"My name's Taviana. I need work and a place to live. Any ideas?"

Her finely plucked eyebrows arch and she tilts her head. "Taviana. That's an unusual name. I've heard it somewhere before." I can see her focusing, trying to make the connection.

Fortunately the guy with the tattoos changes the subject. "You could try the fast-food restaurants. They're usually hiring."

My stomach lurches, remembering lunch. "Thanks, I might have to if nothing else comes up."

"Summer's coming," one of the other guys says. "People will be looking for nannies."

Now that is something I could do, but I can't wait until summer. "Where can I get a local paper?" I ask him. "To check the ads."

"Practically anywhere," he says and points to a convenience store at the end of the block. "You'll find one there for sure."

"Taviana," the girl says, still mulling over my name. "Did you ever live in Highrock?"

My stomach clenches. Will I ever be able to leave my past behind? "Yeah, did you?" Duh.

"Uh-huh, I went to Rockridge School. I think you were there for a while too."

"Maybe." I shrug. "I moved around a lot."

I can't help but notice her smug little smile. The boys will know all about me the minute I walk away. I consider returning to the bus station, collecting my suitcase and catching the first bus to the next town, but chances are they'll know about me there too.

I've lost interest in talking to these guys now that smug-girl is here. "Guess I'll go get a paper then," I tell them. "Maybe it'll list rooms to rent too."

I give a little wave and head toward the road. A moment later a boy jogs up beside me. "I'm going to get a Slurpee," the tattooed guy says. "Mind if I walk with you?"

I glance back at the picnic table. I don't think he stayed long enough to hear about my life in Highrock. Not yet, anyway. "Sure," I say, shrugging. "So, what's your name?"

"Hunter."

"Are those antlers on your arms?"

"Yeah. Do you like them?"

"I'd like them better on a moose."

He laughs. "Me too."

"Do you actually hunt?"

"No. I'm a vegetarian."

I give him a sharp glance. "Are you serious?"

"Yeah." He grins. "Kind of a paradox, isn't it?"

I can't help but smile back at him. His sense of humor is refreshing.

"So if you're not living anywhere, where's your stuff?" he asks.

"In a suitcase at the bus station. If things don't work out here, I can always hop on a bus and try another town."

"Huh. I can't imagine that kind of freedom."

I shrug. "You could do it too."

"No, not really. I want to graduate from school here and go to college in the fall."

"Yeah, well, I'll never graduate from school, so college won't be an option for me."

We're standing outside the convenience store. He's studying me thoughtfully. "It's never too late to go back to school."

"It's kinda hard when you have to support yourself, and when you're already so far behind."

"I bet you could do it," he says.

I smile at him. "Thanks. I like the way you think. But first things first. I need a job and a place to stay."

He holds the door open for me. I grab the free newspaper and wait for him to get a Slurpee. He gets two.

Back outside, he hands me one of the plastic cups, and we wander down the street together until we come to a bus stop. I plunk myself down on the bench and turn to the classified pages. Hunter sits beside me, literally slurping his Slurpee.

"Any luck?" he asks.

I shake my head. "Everyone wants experience, resumes, references. I don't have any of those things."

He sighs. "Something will come up."

I fold the newspaper and slump on the bench. "I hope so." But my mind is already calculating how long my money will hold out. Not long. One or two nights in the cheapest room, maybe. If I don't eat. "I have a connection here who's going to help me out," I tell him, though I'm really just trying to convince myself.

"Who's that?"

"I don't know his name," I admit. "But he helps out the boys who leave Unity. Maybe he even tempts them out. I'm not sure." I think of the Pied Piper again.

"Oh." I see Hunter's expression change. "I think I might know who that is."

"Really?" I sit up, feeling a glimmer of hope.

"Do you want me to see if I can find him?"

"Could you?"

"I'm not exactly sure if I've got the right guy, but my cousin lives next door to this lady who has boys from Unity living with her. My cousin hangs with one of them."

"That would be great."

"Where will you be?"

That stumps me for a moment, but then I realize there's only one place I can go. "The bus depot."

He nods and takes my Slurpee cup from me. "I'll probably be at the park again tomorrow if..." He doesn't finish his sentence.

"Thanks, Hunter. I'll know where to look for you."

"Well, good luck then."

"Thanks for the Slurpee. And for tracking down that guy."

"I haven't found him yet, but I'll see what I can do." He smiles, turns and walks back toward the park.

I head directly to the bus depot, even though it's clear that Hunter won't be able to track the guy down that fast. I can't think of anywhere else to go. The kids at the park will all know about me by now. I won't be going back there, not even to look for Hunter, but I didn't want to tell him that.

I find a seat around the corner from the ticket counter to avoid the stares of the employees.

The afternoon drags on. Buses come and go. I think about Craig and Hunter. In just one afternoon, I've met two really nice guys. Then I remember smug-girl. My heart sinks a little. I hope Hunter won't change his mind about helping me when he finds out about my former life. So much for a fresh start.

When the sky begins to darken, I buy myself a cup of instant soup from a vending machine. It leaves a nasty artificial taste in my mouth. I watch the clock on the wall as the hours slowly move past. A janitor mops the floor and eyes me suspiciously. A bus drops off some people at ten thirty, and when they've left, I am alone in the waiting room. At eleven o'clock, one of the ticket agents comes over to say they are closing until morning and I'll have to move on.

I get my suitcase from the locker and step outside. The spring night is cold so I pull on a hoodie. I consider going back to the park and sleeping on a bench, but I figure the police might patrol there. I don't want to be handed over to social services on my first night here. I turn and walk down the sidewalk in search of an all-night coffee shop where I can pass the hours until the bus depot reopens.

In my former life, before Unity, I spent my evenings working and slept during the day. I usually bunked in with other girls like myself, and we split the rent. With summer coming, I could find places to sleep outside during the daytime…

I give my head a shake, shocked at myself.

A car's headlights momentarily blind me. The car slows when the driver sees me walking down the road, suitcase in hand. The window rolls down. In that instant I'm transported back to Highrock. The man is going to ask *How much?* I'm going to size him up and give him a price. The passenger door will open, and I'll slide in beside him…

"Taviana?" the guy asks.

I'm jolted back to the present. "Yeah." I peer at the face. He looks familiar.

"Remember me? I'm Jimmy. We met the other night. Jon asked me to look for you, and Hunter told me where you'd be."

I sigh and send a silent prayer of thanks to Celeste.

Chapter Eleven

CELESTE

Pain hangs heavy over our home tonight, a massive cloud, ready to burst. Daddy asks us all to meet with him in the big room as soon as the babies have been put to bed. I check in with Mother, but she doesn't feel well enough to make the trip down the stairs. I kiss her cheek and then join the rest of the family. Everyone clutches their hankies.

"Each and every one of us has been saddened by the death of Colleen today," Daddy says when the room becomes quiet. He's standing in front of the floor-to-ceiling window, his hands clasped behind his back. Except for my mother and the babies, each of his wives and all their children are gathered on the furniture or sprawled on the floor. The room is crowded, hot and noisy with sniffling.

"She was a girl who made the supreme sacrifice," he continues in a booming voice, "and she had an unquestioning faith in the Lord. She now resides with Him, in the Kingdom of Heaven. My brother, Jeremy, was most fortunate to have her assigned to him as a plural wife, and he can now look forward to meeting her again in the next life." His speech sounds rehearsed and he's staring beyond us, toward the hallway. I turn and peer down it, but there's nothing there out of the ordinary.

"We know that Colleen was so special to God that he didn't make her earthly stay long or painful," he continues. "She will now assist Him in His work from Heaven, and those of us remaining must figure out how to repent and make atonement for our sins so that we, too, will arrive there." His gaze returns to the room, and he looks about until he sees me. He glares.

I ignore his glare because I'm thinking about his words. If what he says is true, then it would mean that those who are most special will die young. I assume that *special* means those with unquestioning faith. Those who are pure. That counts me out. I glance at Nanette to see if this concerns her, but she is gazing at Daddy with such reverence that I think she's missed the connection altogether.

"Let us pray," Daddy says and bows his head.

I close my eyes and listen as my family recites the Lord's Prayer. If Taviana were here right now, she would take my hand and squeeze it. At one time I would have done the same for Nanette. Now each of us is alone.

At the end of the prayer, Daddy begins reciting a familiar-sounding sermon about how we're the one true church, and how we have kept the principle alive. He reminds us that the principle of plural marriage was God's sacred gift to us. Then he goes on about the second coming of Jesus Christ and how the church must be restored to righteousness. If he thinks he's comforting us in any way, he's fooling himself.

Daddy continues to drone on but eventually notices that his younger children are getting restless, and he wraps it up. "Be sure to remember Colleen's family in your prayers tonight," he says.

"And Taviana," I add brazenly.

The flash of his eyes speaks volumes, but I don't care.

THE NIGHT IS long. Babies cry out, and I hear creaking floorboards as various mothers tend to the smallest children. In our room, Nanette and I are kept busy comforting the little girls. Shortly before dawn, I notice that Rebecca's bed is empty. Alarmed, I check the entire room before padding about the house, wondering where she would go. Eventually I tiptoe into Mother's room and find the two of them snuggled up together, sleeping. I know I should carry her back to her own bed, but they look so peaceful that I tuck the blankets around Rebecca and leave them alone. Like me, the exiling of Taviana is as hard on her as the death of Colleen.

I peek out the window on my way back to bed and notice the sky is beginning to brighten. Knowing that it's almost time to start chores anyway, I decide to stay up and watch the sun come over the mountains. I slip on an old jacket of Daddy's and step out onto the front porch.

The night is still, but as I stand there admiring the shimmering sky, I hear the first bird chirp. It is followed by a second bird and then a third. One by one they welcome the day as the golden, orange and pink hues streak the eastern sky. I sink onto the top step and enjoy the sheer beauty of the sunrise. This is when I feel closest to God, when I truly feel His presence. The stunning display of colors before me is His finest work.

Gradually the colors become bolder, the day lighter, and then the rim of the sun emerges on the horizon, in a valley between two mountain peaks. The chatter of the birds intensifies. The rest of the sun rises more quickly than I imagined it would, and I'm awed as I remember that it's not actually the sun rising but the earth spinning in the universe that creates this illusion.

How I'd love to share this moment with Jon. I know he'd agree with me that God is not in the religious ranting. He is not in the rules, or even in the sacred book. He is here, in the beauty of this divine morning. He is in the music of the birds, in the colors of the sky and even in the goose bumps on my arms. The realization of this makes me dizzy.

I hear the door creak open behind me. Swinging about, I find Pam there, looking as surprised to see me as I am to see her. I move over on the step and pat the space beside me. She smiles shyly and joins me there without a word. We continue to gaze at the miracle in front of us, at the new day unfolding. For a rare moment I feel at peace.

And then the sun is higher, the colors less vivid, and the moment is gone. I glance at Pam's pale face. "Are you okay?"

She nods. "I couldn't sleep."

"Me either."

"I'm really going to miss Taviana," she whispers.

"I know."

"I wanted to talk to your father," she says, "and ask him to find a way for her to stay…"

"But you didn't?"

"No." She sinks a little into herself.

"Why not?"

She looks away. "I'm afraid of him."

I think about that. "Don't the two of you ever talk?"

"Not really."

Poor Pam. This was clearly not a good match on the part of the Prophet. Daddy can be so intimidating, and Pam is so shy, so quiet. I make a mental note to spend more time with her. Maybe that will help each of us miss Taviana a little less.

WASHING MY FACE, I think about the day that lies ahead. The whole community will come out to Colleen's funeral service, and I doubt the Prophet's words will be any more comforting than Daddy's were. I consider staying home to keep Mother company. With all the impure thoughts I've had lately, as well as the lies I've told and the things

I've done, just the thought of entering the church makes me nauscous, but then I change my mind. By going I'll at least be able to see Jon, even from a distance. That thought gives me an instant jolt of excitement.

The chores seem endless. I help make breakfast, do dishes, dress the small children. There is an embroidered and framed proverb on our kitchen wall that says *Many hands make light work*, but I'd say that many hands just mean more people to feed and clean up after.

I guide my little brothers into the church pew while Nanette takes Rebecca and the twins to the child-minding area downstairs. I wait until I see Jon enter the church with his family. They sit in their usual spot, a few pews ahead of us and to the left. When they're settled Jon glances back at me. I smile and nod, and he turns to face forward.

The service is as long and painful as I'd expected. At one point I look across the heads of my brothers to Pam, who is clearly distraught, and no wonder. She is the same age Colleen was. This could just as easily have been her as Colleen. I reach across my brothers and clasp her hand. She squeezes mine back.

It is finally over, and I decide to join the others in the meeting hall after I see that Jon has followed his family downstairs. I keep one eye on him while making polite small talk with other members of the community. I've always hated this kind of socializing. Unlike Nanette, I don't have a set task at these functions. Thank goodness. It means I can usually escape to somewhere quieter.

I glance over at Nanette's serving table and notice that she's having a conversation with Jon's father. There's something about the tilt of her head and the spots of red on her cheeks that seem out of place. He's giving her his undivided attention. Now his hand is on her arm, and he appears to be trying to comfort her. I'd swear there is a flow of energy happening between them, much like the one Jon and I share. Can people stop these things from happening, even though it is clearly wrong? I shake my head and wonder how Nanette and I can be so different. I could never be attracted to an old man like Martin Nielsson. I sigh and wonder how Nanette and I can have grown so far apart in such a short time.

Glancing back at Jon, I see he's been waiting to get my attention. He jerks his head toward the door and then arches his eyebrows. It can only mean one thing. He wants me to leave, to meet him at the river. The usual flutter of excitement stirs up my stomach. I glance about the room, wondering if I can get away with it. Everyone seems preoccupied, still lost in conversations. I figure I should be able to disappear for at least a little while.

I nod and smile. Jon smiles back. A moment later I climb the stairs and start down the road.

❦ Chapter Twelve ❦

Nanette

"It's a very sad day, isn't it, Nanette," Martin Nielsson says, picking up a glass of juice from my table after Colleen's funeral.

I nod but can't make eye contact with him. The dreams I've been having about the two of us are fresh in my mind, and to actually speak with him, well, it feels…sinful. Especially today.

"At least the baby has other mothers to care for her."

I glance around at the women who are clustered in groups. Most of them have red-rimmed eyes or are still mopping at their faces with handkerchiefs. Colleen's tiny baby is being cradled by Ruth, Uncle Jeremy's first wife.

"And I hear Taviana has left Unity."

"Yes, she has."

"Is your family missing her?"

"No," I tell him. "We know that it was for the best. Taviana did not belong here." I'm proud of my mature response.

When I finally get the courage to glance at him, his head is tilted and he's frowning.

"Don't you agree?" I ask him.

He doesn't answer immediately. When he does, he speaks slowly. "I thought Taviana was an asset to our community," he says. "Through her, we were reminded that this is a preferable place to live."

"Father and I believe she was putting impure thoughts into Celeste's head."

"Oh. Well, that is a problem."

"And she was prone to telling stories."

"Stories?"

"Inappropriate stories."

"I see."

He stands quietly for a moment. I keep my hands busy by wiping up the spills on the table.

"How is your mother, Nanette? I haven't seen her in church for a while."

"She's…" What do I say? I can't talk to a man about her health. "She's not too good."

"Oh dear. I'm sorry to hear that."

I nod and feel my eyes filling with tears again.

"Nanette, what is it?" Mr. Nielsson is leaning toward me, concerned.

I try to blink back the tears, but it's been an emotional day, and they're so close to the surface. I can feel my lip quivering.

"Nanette?"

I let it spill. "I'm scared that the same thing is going to happen to my mother as happened to Colleen."

"Oh, Nanette. Your mother has given birth to many children. She will be fine."

I can only shrug and wipe my eyes. I can't tell him that she too had bleeding.

He reaches out and touches my arm gently. "It's in God's hands, child. He will take care of her."

"Where was God for Colleen?" I ask, and then, shocked at myself, I drop my face into my hands.

His hand continues to linger on my arm. I pull it away and feel my cheeks burn. He straightens his shoulders and adjusts his shirt collar.

"What has become of your faith, child?" he asks.

I shrug. "Maybe I've been spending too much time with Celeste."

He regards me thoughtfully. "Spend some time with the sacred book, Nanette, and practice purity. You'll be fine."

I nod but can no longer look at him. Why did he leave his hand on my arm so long?

"Tragic events like Colleen's death often make us question our faith, Nanette. It is normal. You'll feel better in a few days and be as faithful as ever again. Trust me, child."

I look up at him and try to smile. He gives me a sad smile in return.

"Good day, then, Nanette," he says and, with a last glance at me, walks away from the table.

What have I done? Does he think I'm a stupid child now? I take a deep breath and exhale slowly.

People are beginning to drift away from the hall. I look around and see Celeste standing alone in one corner.

She has a small smile on her face. I glance across the room to see who it is that she's smiling at. It's Jon Nielsson, and he's smiling back at her. I turn to see Celeste nod. Then Jon nods too. When I look back to Celeste, she's climbing the stairs to leave. I watch Jon. He waits a few minutes, but then he too heads up the stairs.

I fill a few more glasses with juice. Then I abandon my table and climb the stairs myself. Stepping out of the church, I look down the road and see Jon walking in the direction of the river. There is no sign of Celeste. An uneasy feeling settles over me.

I go back into the church and help round up my younger brothers and sisters. Most of them were in the child-minding room during the service. With a twin on each hip and Rebecca at my side, I join the rest of the family on the front lawn and we walk home together. It's a quiet group, and Father seems preoccupied. Once again, there is no sign of Celeste.

After the children have been fed and the little ones have been put down for naps, I take a tray of food to my mother. Her mood has been particularly bleak since Colleen's death. Colleen was her cousin.

"Mr. Nielsson asked about you after the service," I tell her.

"That was kind of him," she says. She's holding a sandwich but hasn't taken a single bite of it yet. Her eyes are dark, empty.

"Faith is walking around the coffee table now." I keep talking, trying to distract her. "Joan pulls herself up on the table, but she hasn't taken any steps yet."

Mother nods and puts the sandwich back on the plate. "Thank you, Nanette, but I'm really not hungry today."

I wrack my brain for something else to say. What would Taviana have done? "Would you like me to read to you from the book?" I ask.

"No, I think I need to sleep some more. I feel so tired today."

How can she sleep anymore? It's all she does. "Okay." I pick up the tray and begin to leave the room, but then I remember what I want to talk to her about. I return to my chair beside her bed and place the tray on the side table. "Mother..."

"Hmmm." Her eyes are already closed.

"There's something I'm worried about."

She forces her eyes to open again, but her lids are droopy and she barely focuses on me. "What is it, Nanette?" she asks.

"I think Celeste is seeing a boy, secretly."

She tries to sit up a little bit. "What makes you think this?"

"Well, she's been disappearing a lot lately. And today I saw her smiling at a boy in the church hall, and then they both left, separately. She hasn't come home since the service."

She lies back again and sighs. "She'll be married soon enough. Let's not say anything about this to your father. It will only get him upset, and he has enough to worry about."

I stare at her, shocked. "Mother! She will not be pure for her husband."

"We don't know that for sure, Nanette. Maybe she's just in need of some alone time."

"But…"

"Let it go, Nanette. Her life will be filled with her own responsibilities all too soon. We can allow her a little freedom for this short time."

I think my mother's condition has affected her thinking. Or maybe it's the double shock of losing both Taviana and Colleen in the same day. I pick up the tray and storm out of the room, more determined now than ever to tell Father what Celeste is up to, but first I have to find out for sure. Father has no patience for rumors that are not based on concrete evidence.

Pam is still washing up the dishes in the kitchen. I drop the tray on the counter and tell her that Mother has given me a message to deliver to Ruth, Uncle Jeremy's wife. Pam simply nods and carries on.

I slip into outdoor shoes and hurry along the road. I can see men out working in the fields, and a few women are outside hanging laundry or pulling weeds in their gardens, but no one pays any attention to me.

Passing the playground where we often take the children after school, I carry on down to the river and then head upstream. I have only walked a short way when I see them.

CELESTE

I arrive at the river before Jon, so I pick my way across the beach to the stone people. One more has been added to the family, and it stands close to the stone woman I built a few days ago. My heart swells. This game that we are playing fills me with an unexplainable delight, and I wish I had time to build another one right away.

When I see Jon crossing the beach, I run toward the knoll of trees where we've been meeting. He greets me with a hug. "I have good news," he says.

"Really?"

"Yep. Do you want to guess what it is?"

I shrug. "Does it have to do with Taviana?"

"It does."

"What?"

"Guess."

"Jimmy found her a place to live?"

"He did."

I give Jon a quick hug. Considering I rarely ever hugged anyone two weeks ago, it's sure coming easily to me now. "Great! Where?"

"There's a lady who lives in Springdale. She left Unity years ago and now takes in boys who want to leave and start a new life."

Something about this sounds vaguely familiar. "Is her name Abigail?"

"Yeah."

My heart sinks. I remember hearing the women in my house talk in whispers about Abigail. According to the gossip, she ran off in the middle of the night with her five children. The whole community was shocked. Her husband tracked her down and rescued the children, bringing them safely back to Unity, but she wouldn't come. Clearly she was mentally unstable to do such a thing. Devil's work, the mothers said. How could she not come back and raise her own children?

"Are you sure that's a good idea?"

"A good idea? To live with Abigail?"

"Yeah, I heard she's…not quite right."

Jon frowns. "You heard she's not right because she chose to leave Unity, right?"

I see where he's going with this. "No, because she chose not to raise her own children."

"I'm sure she *wanted* to raise her children, just not in Unity. We don't know why she ran away. Maybe she couldn't live with her husband."

"His other wives manage just fine."

"Maybe they stay because the same thing would happen to them—they'd lose their children if they tried to leave."

I'm still doubtful. "How does Abigail live? What does she do for money?"

"She works. She said Taviana can stay as long as she needs to, as long as she obeys the house rules."

"I don't know..."

"Celeste, Abigail has saved Taviana from sleeping on the streets. Isn't that what you wanted?"

It was. "You're right." I suddenly realize how ungrateful I must sound. "Thanks, Jon." I lean into him, and he kisses me. It only takes me a few seconds to forget my worries as Jon's lips move softly across mine. My mind and body swirl away again, taking me to that place of combined contentment and longing, a place far from the mundane sameness of my days. I want to stay here forever.

The crunch of scraping rocks jolts me back to the present. I spin around and find Nanette standing there, her hand covering her mouth, her eyes bulging.

Our eyes lock and we stare at each other for a moment. Then she whirls around and runs off.

"Nanette!" I holler and start to chase her, but she doesn't pause, and she's faster than I am. I stop to catch my breath. A coldness surges through me, as though my blood has turned to ice water.

"Where will she go?" Jon asks, coming up behind me.

At first I can't talk. My mouth opens, but my throat is dry. I swallow. "Straight to Father," I rasp.

Jon comes around to face me. He frowns. "What will he do?"

I shrug. "Lock me in my room until I'm married, I guess." I'm still trying to get a grip on my physical reaction. Now my hands are shaking, but my body feels numb.

"Celeste." Jon suddenly reaches out both his hands and grabs mine. His eyes are wide. "Let's leave right now. Together. Abigail will take us in too, I'm sure of it."

I yank my hands away. "You can't be serious."

"I've never been more serious." His hands are now clenched into fists at his sides.

"I can't leave my family," I tell him. "This is where I belong."

"You'll be leaving your family when you're married, which will be soon. This is your chance to change the direction of your life."

I just stare at him, trying to keep my balance. I'm feeling sicker by the minute.

"C'mon, Celeste. You know you don't want this life."

"I also know I cannot disgrace my family. That would kill me."

"But being a sister wife with lots of babies won't kill you? I don't believe that."

"Just because Colleen died doesn't mean…"

"I don't mean kill you physically. I mean it will kill your spirit. There will be no more rock men when you're married, no more thinking outside the box. Your life will be identical to every other woman in Unity, and I think you want more than that."

"Jon, you don't understand…"

"I understand perfectly. You care more about your family's reputation than you do about yourself. But Celeste, I have to leave right now. When your father finds out who you were with, I will be banished anyway. I'm going to be gone before that happens. I want you to come with me."

"Jon…"

"We need to leave now."

"I can't."

He just stares at me.

"I'm so sorry."

Jon's expression has turned hard. I know he is disappointed in me, but he doesn't understand what this would do to my father, my mother, my entire family. He makes one last attempt to convince me. "Come with me, Celeste, before it's too late."

I shake my head, panicky. "Please don't go, Jon," I plead. "My life will be empty without you."

"I have no choice."

I know he's right, but I can't face it.

He regards me some more. Finally he shrugs. "Good-bye, Celeste." He turns and starts walking away from me, away from Unity.

"No, Jon! Wait!" I run up behind him and grab his hand. He turns, and I see tears in his eyes. He pulls his hand away and shakes his head. Then he starts walking again. He stumbles once but straightens himself, throws his shoulders back and does not turn around again.

I watch until he rounds a bend in the river and I can't see him anymore.

JUST AS I knew he would, Father has ordered me to remain in the house. I have no problem with that. I have nowhere to go now anyway.

When he hauled me into his office after I returned from the beach, his anger was like a summer storm, a sudden crash of elements. The room was electrified by his fury, and I wanted to cower in a corner. But, unlike the aftermath of a summer storm, the air was not left freshened when it was over. It was full of tension, and the pain I felt was a physical ache, not because of the anger I caused my father but from the pain of losing Jon.

Father forbids me to join the family at the evening meal. I guess he wants to tell everyone what a disgraceful person I am, so I spend the afternoon and evening in the girls' bedroom, flopped on Taviana's cot, which has not yet been put away. Pulling the scratchy blanket over my shoulders, I wonder why she never complained. The cot sags in the middle, and the blanket is stiff. I'm tempted to lie on my own bed, but it reminds me too much of Nanette, my traitorous sister.

I flip onto my side. If Taviana were here, I could tell her about Jon and how we feel about each other. She would understand how confused I am—loving Jon but not being able to leave Unity. I could tell her how angry he seemed.

She would find something to say to make me feel better, or she'd tell me a story and make me laugh...

AT BREAKFAST IT becomes clear that all the women know of my...my *indiscretion*, as Daddy called it. I get sour looks from Lena and Deborah. Nanette is avoiding me completely. I try to make eye contact with Pam, but she appears lost in her own little world, as always.

I take a tray of food up to Mother and find her resting in bed, staring into space.

"Celeste!" she says, clearly pleased to see me. This is a relief. I wondered if she, too, was going to give me the silent treatment. "Happy birthday!"

Her words startle me. I'd completely forgotten the date.

"Thank you. I'd...I'd forgotten." I place the tray on the table beside her bed and sit down beside her.

"Will you bring Rebecca up to see me later?" she asks. "I want to wish her a happy birthday too."

I nod.

She pulls herself up to a sitting position, and reaches for my hand. "I heard you got into a little trouble yesterday."

Tears prick my eyes, and I blink them away. I decide to be honest with her. "I really...like him, and I don't want to marry anyone else."

She sighs and then squeezes my hand even tighter. "I liked a boy too, before your father."

"You did?" This news shocks me.

"Well, I didn't spend time alone with him, like I hear you did with your boy." She tilts her head, studying my face. I look down at my hands, not willing to confess too much. "But we noticed each other, that's for sure. I used to lie awake at night, thinking of him and wishing we could be together."

"I've done that too."

"I suspect most girls have a boy they dream about."

I'm astounded to discover that I'm not the only one with impure thoughts, but then I remember my sister. I shake my head. "Not Nanette. She's perfect."

Mother laughs a little. "I doubt that. Though she certainly works hard at it."

We sit in silence for a moment.

"But just because you like a boy, Celeste, doesn't mean the Lord has it in His plan for you to be together. The man you'll be assigned to will take care of you and provide you with a home. A mere boy could never do that."

"I'd be happy to stay here. I'm not ready for children and sister wives."

"Celeste," she says softly, picking at a broken thread on her quilt. "It's amazing how fast you'll adjust. Change is hard, but you're a wise girl, and you know that here we sacrifice our childish whims in order to obtain a place in God's kingdom. You'll find the happiness you long for in the heart of your new family."

I'm watching my mother's face as she speaks, and I notice that the haunting sadness of her eyes does not match her words. I also know that in her own way she's telling me she won't listen to any more talk about Jon.

"Eat your breakfast, Mother," I tell her. "The baby needs his nourishment."

"You think it's going to be a boy?" she asks, reaching for a piece of toast.

"The last three were girls. A boy would balance things out."

She nods. I wait quietly while she eats. I'd like to ask her more—how she felt when she was assigned to Daddy, how long it took Lena to accept her, and who the boy was that she longed for. I wonder if he still lives in Unity and if she ever thinks about him. But I remain silent, knowing that I would be asking too much of her.

When she's finished eating, she slides back down into bed and I tuck the blankets around her.

"Are they giving you a rough time?" she asks.

"Pardon me?"

"Lena and Deborah."

"Oh. That. Yeah, well, they're letting me know they think I'm evil."

"You're not evil, Celeste." She sighs. "And it's your birthday. If I could, I'd get up and relieve you of some of your chores to give you a break."

"I know you would." I place my hand on hers.

She gets a dreamy look on her face. "I remember so clearly the day you were born. My first child. You were like a miracle to me—so tiny and precious. I wouldn't let anyone else hold you or even change your diaper. I was too afraid they'd drop you or something."

I smile at her, wishing I could remember when I was her only child. Now she's expecting her eighth, and she's just turning thirty-two.

"And now you're fifteen, and the cycle continues. I wonder if my mother felt this way when her oldest daughter turned fifteen."

"How do you feel?" I ask.

"Proud." She smiles. "And sad that you won't be living here much longer. But excited too, knowing we're on the right path, heading toward the highest degree of celestial glory."

"Speaking of chores," I tell her, ignoring this religious talk, "I better get back at it. I'm in enough trouble around here."

"How mad was your father?"

"Very."

"He wants what is right for you, Celeste. That's all."

I simply nod, not wanting to aggravate her. But deep down, I now realize that what Daddy actually wants is what is right for *him*. Nobody ever asked me if being a celestial wife is right for me. If they had, I'd have told them no.

❧ *Chapter Fourteen* ❧

Taviana

A bigail studies me from her rocking chair. She reminds me of an overgrown bulldog who is especially grouchy about being woken in the middle of the night by a pesky intruder. I'm the intruder.

Jimmy brought me straight to Abigail's Freedom House, as he calls it, after rescuing me off the street. He'd left me standing alone in the dark living room with my suitcase while he went to wake her up. It felt totally wrong, and I'd begged him to just let me sleep on the couch until morning, but he said that was against house rules, and no one dared break house rules. Abigail had lumbered into the room, tying the sashes of her housecoat around her thick waist, her long braid tousled from sleep. She'd switched on a couple of lamps, glanced at me with half-asleep eyes and then disappeared into the kitchen. I heard the sound of water running, possibly a kettle being filled, and a murmur of conversation with Jimmy, who'd followed her in there.

When she came back into the living room, she'd motioned for me to sit on the couch, and she sank into the rocking chair.

Now she rubs her face with her hands in an attempt to come fully awake. When she finally speaks, her voice is weary. "Hello, Taviana."

I nod.

"I've been expecting you."

That startles me. "You have?"

She sighs heavily. "Yes, I have."

"Why?"

She ignores my question but says, "I'm surprised you lasted there as long as you did."

I find myself squirming in my chair. "I liked it there. It was safe."

"You don't have to live in Unity to be safe."

"I did."

"Only because you didn't know you had other choices."

I hear the whistling of a kettle. "Jimmy," she says. He's leaning against the doorjamb leading to the kitchen, arms crossed. "Make the tea, please." Then she eyes me intently. "When was the last time you ate anything?"

I think about the pathetic cup of soup I had at the bus station, but before I can answer, she says, "Scramble up some eggs for her too."

"Scrambled eggs, coming right up."

He disappears into the kitchen and she settles herself into the chair. "Okay, from the beginning. Tell me how you got here."

I know she isn't asking how I got from the bus depot to her house, and her no-nonsense attitude works like a truth serum. I sit back and describe life with my mother, living on the streets, and how I met Jacob and ended up living in Unity. "And everything was fine until the Prophet ordered me to leave," I conclude.

Jimmy comes into the living room and hands us each a mug of tea.

"That Jacob is a special one," she says, warming her hands on her mug. "Even if he is one of them."

I nod, thinking of him, and wonder how well she knows the people there.

"So now what?" Abigail asks me.

The question takes me by surprise. Somehow I'd expected *her* to tell *me* what would happen next.

"Now I hope to find work and a place to live."

She doesn't reply.

"A real job," I explain, in case she misunderstood. "Not what I was doing before."

Jimmy comes back in and hands me a plate heaping with scrambled eggs and toast. It smells delicious. He also hands me cutlery and then sits on the couch beside me.

"Thanks," I say, and suddenly I realize how hungry I am. I place the plate on the coffee table in front of me, lean over it and begin shoveling food into my mouth.

"In case you're wondering," Abigail says, "Jimmy received a phone call today from someone who lives in Unity, so we knew you were in town but we couldn't figure out where you might go. Tonight, after I was in bed, there was a knock on the door and a young man was there."

"Hunter."

"Yeah, that's right," Jimmy said. "Apparently he'd been trying to find a phone number for me but gave up and just came over."

Celeste, Jon and Hunter. I owe each of them.

"You'd better get to bed, Jimmy," Abigail tells him. He nods, gives me a reassuring smile and disappears down the hall. Abigail waits until I've finished my eggs. Then she places her mug on a table beside her. She leans forward. "So, what about school?" she asks.

"What about it?"

"Aren't you planning to finish it?"

"No, I'm too far behind."

"It's hard to find a decent job without a high school diploma."

"I'm sure I can find something. I'm a hard worker."

"If you're a hard worker, you can finish school."

I think about the kids I met in the park today. Smuggirl will have told them all about what I did in Highrock. "I can't go back to school," I tell her simply. "I'm not like the rest of them."

"We can't keep running from past mistakes," Abigail says. "At some point, we need to accept what is, what was done, and move on."

Easier said than done, I think, and I then remember the book I wanted to borrow from the library today, how the jacket blurb said the character was haunted by her past. I wonder how she ended up finding redemption. I definitely need to read that book.

"How old are you, Taviana?" Abigail asks.

"I just turned seventeen."

She shakes her head. "You've seen a lot in your seventeen years. Going from living on the street to Unity... that's going from one extreme to another."

"It is." I nod. "But I needed that extreme. It was the only way I could break the pattern of my life."

Abigail studies me. I look around the room. It is small and overcrowded with furniture, but it feels homey. There are pictures of children all over the room.

"So what do you know about me?" she asks suddenly.

"Not much. Just that you took in Jimmy and some other boys who decided to leave Unity."

"Did you know that my children still live there?"

"No." That surprises me.

She sighs but doesn't share any more details. "So here's the deal," she says, folding her arms across her chest. "I take in young people who have left Unity and need a place to live. It's always been boys in the past, but I'm happy to provide a home for girls too." She clears her throat. "The authorities recognize the service I provide for these kids, so they turn a blind eye when it comes to laws about legal guardianship and all that."

I nod.

"But there are rules. If you are willing to follow the rules, you are welcome to live here."

"I got pretty used to rules in Unity."

"Yes, I guess you did. But mine are different."

I wait for her to continue.

"Rule number one. You must attend high school until you graduate."

"But I just told you that I can't do that!"

She shrugs.

I cross my arms and sit back. I should have known that this was too good to be true.

"Do you want to hear the other rules?"

"Whatever."

"Everyone pitches in with the cooking and cleaning. I provide a place for you to live, but it's not a hotel. The curfew is ten thirty on school nights, midnight on weekends. If you can, I encourage you to work part-time while you attend school so you can contribute to your keep. I expect common courtesy and good manners at all times. We respect each other's belongings and we each attend a church service of our choice."

I must look surprised at that because she explains. "I may have left Unity, but I did not lose my faith in a higher power. It is my hope that the members of this family—and that's what we are, a family—will find strength in God's love, just as I do.

"This is also not a flop house," she continues. "If you bring someone over to sleep, you check with me first, as Jimmy did tonight." She thinks for a moment. "It hasn't been an issue in the past," she says, "because there have been only boys, but of course boys and girls will occupy separate bedrooms. Occasionally we have to double up."

I suddenly feel incredibly tired. The rules sound about the same as they did in the group homes I lived in before, and those never worked out for me.

"Any questions, Taviana?"

I notice a slight change in her voice. It's somewhat softer, gentler. Even her face looks less bulldoggish now.

I shake my head.

"You're welcome to take a couple of days to think about it."

"But I already know I can't go back to school."

"We can get you help with your schoolwork, if that's what you're worried about."

"It's not."

She sighs. "I didn't think so. Now listen," she says in her gentler voice. "I can see you're exhausted. Things always look better after a good night's sleep. In the morning you can meet the boys, and I'll give you until Saturday to decide what you're going to do."

She's right. I am exhausted. I decide to accept her hospitality for tonight, and maybe for a few more days. With any luck I will have found myself a job and another place to live by Saturday.

THE SOUND OF male laughter and clanging dishes drags me from a deep sleep. It takes a moment to remember where I am, but when I do I get up and quickly pull on my clothes. I comb my hair with my fingers before I step into the hallway. The coast is clear. I duck into the bathroom and then head down the hall toward the kitchen.

Sitting at the table are Jimmy and two other boys. Abigail is standing at the counter making sandwiches. Jimmy smiles when he sees me. "Morning, Taviana," he says.

I smile. "Hey."

"This is Matthew and Selig."

They both smile shyly, nod and continue eating. They look like so many of the boys I saw in Unity, with their sandy-colored hair and wiry bodies. I wonder what gave them the courage to leave.

"How are you feeling this morning?" Abigail asks. She's wrapping two heaping sandwiches at a time in plastic wrap. These boys must have big appetites.

"Good, thanks," I reply.

"That's great," she says. "So, Jimmy and I are off to work, and Matthew and Selig are off to school. The house is all yours until school gets out."

I nod. "Is there anything you need done?"

Abigail looks surprised that I asked. "Thank you. I suppose you could clean up the kitchen when we're done."

"No problem." I pull out a chair beside Jimmy's and reach for a piece of toast from a plate that's stacked high with them. "Where do you work?" I ask him.

"I'm on a construction crew. We're all over the place, wherever there's work." He takes two more pieces of toast and reaches for the jar of homemade jam.

"Have you finished school?"

"Yep." He glances at Abigail, who is piling fruit, water bottles and cookies on the counter beside the sandwiches. "House rules. And I'm going to trade school in the fall. I'm just saving up money in the meantime."

I spread peanut butter on my toast. The room has grown painfully quiet since I arrived. "So," I say, turning to the other boys, "what grade are you guys in?"

"I'm in eleven," Selig answers. "He's in twelve." Matthew nods.

"And you both lived in Unity before?"

They each nod, but no one offers anything else. What happened to the laughter that woke me up a few minutes ago?

When they're finished their breakfast, Selig and Matthew take their dishes to the sink, rinse them and put them in the dishwasher. They grab their backpacks, which are hanging on hooks in the front hall, and fill them with the sandwiches and snacks that Abigail has put out.

Jimmy is filling a thermos with tea, and Abigail is putting the lunch makings away. "I'll do that," I tell her. "You get ready for work."

"They trained you well in Unity," she says, smiling. "Thank you."

Once again I see a hint of softness in her weathered face. Perhaps I judged her too harshly last night. I suppose I wouldn't be at my best either if I were dragged out of my bed in the middle of the night. She takes her mug and heads down the hall.

As I finish tidying up the kitchen, Jimmy hangs behind, watching me.

"We all still have family in Unity," he says.

I nod.

"We miss them."

"Oh." I hadn't thought about that.

"Selig's only been here a few months. I think he's pretty homesick. We try to keep his mind off his family."

I nod. "I'll try to remember that."

"A few of them end up returning, even though they know they want more than they can ever have there."

"Why would they go back?" I take the dishrag and wipe down the table.

"Guilt. Love. Sometimes it's just too hard to break the ties."

"Hmm. I wouldn't know. I've never really had a family. The one I lived with in Unity was as close as I ever got."

"Then stick with us," he says cheerfully. "We may not be related through blood, but...sometimes the family you choose is easier to live with than the one you were given."

I smile as best I can but don't try to explain that it's not going to work for me. There's no way I'm going back to school.

I wander around the house, picking up the pictures, wondering about the faces peering out of them. I notice that the dusting hasn't been done for a while, so I find a rag in the laundry room and get to work. Then I decide that I should vacuum as well. When that's done, I turn on the TV and flick through the channels. It's been a long time since

I've done this, but not much has changed. There's nothing on but commercials, old movies and talk shows at this time of day. None of it interests me. I flick it off.

I rifle through my suitcase, looking for something appropriate to wear for job hunting. There's nothing, and everything I do have smells stale. I put a load in the washing machine and then pace around the house some more.

Finding myself back in the kitchen, I take a quick inventory of food. The cupboards and fridge are well stocked. Thinking about the appetites of those boys, I pull out a large mixing bowl and gather the ingredients I need to make a batch of muffins. Learning to cook was something good that came out of my time in Unity. I was always happy when I was assigned to kitchen work.

When the muffins are baking, I combine ingredients for a meat loaf and put it in the fridge for later.

After cleaning up the kitchen and putting my clothes in the drier, I go outside and take a look around the backyard. The sun is warm, and I plunk down into a lawn chair and think about how nice it is to be living in a home instead of a rented room somewhere.

I'm folding my clean clothes and putting them away when Selig and Matthew bang through the door. My heart leaps, and I rush into the hall. "Hi!"

My overenthusiastic greeting embarrasses them. "Hi," Selig says, turning beet red and not making eye contact with me. He hangs his backpack on a hook. Matthew just grunts a greeting and walks toward the kitchen, giving me a wide berth.

"I made muffins," I say, still over the top with enthusiasm. What has gotten into me?

That interests them. Matthew takes the margarine out of the fridge, and they sit at the table with the basket of muffins in front of them.

"How was school?" I ask, parentlike, even though I'm the same age as Matthew.

"Good," they say in unison, their mouths full.

Matthew slathers margarine on a second one. "Have you already graduated?" he asks.

I place a jug of milk on the table. "Yep, I'm finished." My half-truth hangs in the air between us. I decide to come clean. "But not graduated."

Selig frowns. "Abigail's bending the rules for you?"

"Nope. She's giving me a week to find somewhere else to go."

"Why don't you just come to school with us?" he asks. "It's not so bad."

I reach for a muffin now too. "It would be bad for me."

He shrugs and pours himself a second glass of milk. "I thought I'd get slagged when the kids found out where I'm from," he says. "But everyone's been all right. We even get invited to hang out on weekends. The first time I got invited to someone's place, I thought maybe I was getting set up or something. But it was cool."

I remember the guy in the park who referred to Unity as Rabbitsville. Maybe not all the kids are like that.

Matthew collapses on the couch in the living room and flicks on the TV while Selig spreads out his books on the kitchen table. I pick up the novel he's pulled out of his bag and read the back flap. "Is this any good?" I ask him.

"Yeah, it's okay," he says. "But I have to do a project on it, which I'm dreading. I'm not a big reader."

Well duh. He comes from Unity. "Do you mind if I read it for a bit?"

"Sure, go ahead. I've got other homework to do first."

I take the book down the hall to my bedroom and stretch out on my bed. This is heaven.

When Jimmy arrives home, I realize that I've been reading for over an hour. I get up to greet him. "Hi, Taviana!" he says, smiling broadly. I smile back, surprised at how happy I am to see him. He devours two muffins before locking himself in the bathroom to shower. I preheat the oven and scrub some potatoes. Then I slide them into the oven with the meat loaf and slice up some tomatoes and cucumber. I toss them with lettuce and put the bowl of salad in the fridge. I join Selig at the table and read while he does his homework.

"Something smells wonderful in here," Abigail comments when she gets home.

"Taviana made a meat loaf," Matthew says, joining us in the kitchen.

"And muffins," Selig adds.

"And I think the house has been cleaned too," Abigail says, looking around.

I nod, glad that she noticed.

"Thanks, honey," she says. "This is a real treat to come home to."

"You're welcome."

The phone rings, and I hear Jimmy stomping into the living room to pick it up. Abigail peers into the fridge. "Wow," she says. "You have been busy."

"I had to do something."

"No job hunting?"

"No. I decided to wash all my clothes, and then I realized that I don't own anything that's appropriate for job hunting."

Abigail just nods thoughtfully.

"I've got a bit of money, so maybe I'll go buy something new tomorrow," I tell her. "Unless you want it to cover my room and board here."

"No, no. I'm sure you're long overdue for some new clothes. And you certainly earned your keep today."

Jimmy comes back into the kitchen with a goofy grin on his face. "Have I got a surprise for you," he tells me.

"You do?"

"Uh-huh."

"What is it?"

"I'm not telling. You'll have to wait." He turns to Abigail. "We need to talk, alone."

"Down to my room then," Abigail says.

Jimmy gives me another cheeky grin and follows Abigail down the hall. I open up my book and continue reading.

AFTER DINNER, MATTHEW and Selig load the dishwasher and begin doing the dishes. When I offer to help them, Abigail pushes me into the living room. "We share the work around here," she says. "You cooked, they can clean up."

I settle myself on the couch with the book. Boys never helped with the housework in Unity. This will take some getting used to.

I watch as Abigail hands Jimmy the car keys. "Come straight home," she tells him.

"Where are you going?" I ask.

"To collect your surprise," he tells me.

I shake my head, smiling, and continue reading.

"Is that Selig's book?" Abigail asks.

I nod.

"When did you start reading it?"

"This afternoon."

"You're a fast reader."

I glance down and notice that I'm about halfway through. "It's a good book."

"Maybe you'll be able to help Selig with his project."

"Yeah, maybe." I remember a favor I want to ask. "Would it be okay with you if I give your address on my library card application?"

"Absolutely."

"Thanks." Now I will definitely make the trip into town tomorrow.

The house grows quiet as Matthew and Selig do homework and Abigail sits at a desk that's pushed into a corner of the living room. She sorts through papers. I get so caught up in Selig's novel that I don't realize it's getting dark until Abigail switches on a lamp beside me.

Suddenly the front door bangs open and Jimmy steps inside. "Are you ready for your surprise?" he asks me.

I nod and smile.

He moves aside and motions to someone still standing on the doorstep. "C'mon in."

A moment later, Jon steps into the living room. He looks around and when he sees me, he smiles. "Hi, Taviana," he says.

❋ Chapter Fifteen ❋

CELESTE

I feel like a caged animal. My head is spinning with whining babies and bossy sister wives. I'm not even permitted to go into the yard to tend to the garden or hang laundry on the line, and the weather is beautiful. Through the window I can see the new leaves on the trees quivering in a light breeze. Taviana once described a day like this as luscious. I'm missing her stories and funny words even more than I thought I would. She was such a wonderful diversion from the endlessly boring housework. I want to be outside, filling my lungs with fresh air, feeling the heat of the sun on my face. I want to be at the river, building an inuksuk with Jon.

As I wipe sticky fingerprints off the front window, I see a lone male figure coming down the driveway. I watch as he gets closer. It's Martin Nielsson, Jon's father! He veers off the driveway and crosses the side yard, heading to the barn where Daddy is working today. My heart pounds in my chest.

I'm scrubbing so hard at the window my arm aches. Vinegar fumes burn my eyes. Now I see my father marching across the yard toward the house, his face stormy. My stomach lurches when the back door slams open. "Celeste!"

I drop my rag and spray bottle and hurry to the backroom. "Yes, Daddy?"

He simply grabs my sore arm and hauls me across the yard to the barn. He pushes me into his office, where Mr. Nielsson is waiting. I look from one to the other.

"My son is gone," Mr. Nielsson says, his voice ragged.

"Because of you," Daddy spits out.

I stare at my feet.

"He is my first born, my strongest and brightest boy," Mr. Nielsson says. "He works hard on the farm. His mother is beside herself with grief. We need him home."

"What do you say for yourself, Celeste?" my father rages.

My hands tremble and my mind goes blank. I have no idea how to answer him.

"Celeste, say something!" he orders.

I can only shake my head. I have no words.

Daddy turns abruptly and grabs the leather strap off the wall. He yanks it down. I step back and feel my mouth drop open.

Mr. Nielsson places his hand on Daddy's arm. "Let me talk to her, Kelvin."

Daddy pulls his arm away from Mr. Nielsson. He's exhaling in short puffs and his eyes are on fire. I can see from his expression that he's trying to come to some kind of decision. He grips the strap. Clutch, release. Clutch, release.

Suddenly his arm is in the air and the strap comes down hard, smacking the desk. I jump. "She's all yours, for ten minutes," he growls. "If she hasn't said something, at least apologized, by the time I get back…"

He doesn't finish the sentence, but we all know exactly what the threat is. "I don't care how old you are," he says to me. "You've disgraced this family."

Daddy storms out of the office, and I'm left alone with Mr. Nielsson. I glance at his face, expecting to see the same fury as was on Daddy's, but he's only watching me sadly.

"Let's sit down," he suggests.

We sit in two chairs, facing each other. My hands are still trembling. I take a deep breath. "I'm sorry Jon left, Mr. Nielsson," I say. I hadn't realized that it was an apology Daddy was looking for.

"I'm sure you are," Mr. Nielsson says gently. "And I know you're not completely responsible for what happened. Jon was equally to blame, but I'd forgive him completely if he'd come back before the rest of the community finds out."

"He was planning to leave Unity anyway," I tell him. "It just happened a little sooner."

Mr. Nielsson sits back, surprised. "Are you sure? He was always obedient. A good boy."

"I'm sure. He told me he was questioning his faith, that he had been for some time."

"I didn't know." He shakes his head.

We sit in silence for a while. Then he asks, "Do you know where he is?"

I shake my head and straighten my apron. I do know, but I'm not telling. Besides, it wouldn't take much for him to figure it out anyway.

I guess he knows that too. "If I did find him, do you think I could convince him to come home?" he asks me.

Now I look directly at him. "No."

I see him slump in his chair. I know exactly what he's going through.

"Not even to see you?" he asks.

I shake my head.

"How do you feel about that?" he asks, finally.

I simply shrug. I'm sure he knows the truth, that I'm as devastated as he is, but there's no point in admitting my impure thoughts.

"Celeste, I know what it's like to be attracted to someone…someone that the Prophet hasn't assigned to me," Mr. Nielsson says quietly.

I glance at him, shocked that he'd admit this to me. Shocked that he also has impure thoughts. His eyes don't meet mine.

We sit in silence. I want to say something, but the words don't come. Then I hear the barn door creak open and my father's footsteps stomping down the corridor.

"I'll tell your father that we've had a good discussion," he whispers. "And if Jon somehow contacts you, or gets a message to you, please, Celeste, tell him how much we miss him."

Now our eyes do meet. I'm startled that he thinks I may hear from Jon.

"Okay?" he asks.

I simply nod, and Daddy storms into the room. "Well?" he demands.

Mr. Nielsson gets to his feet. "Celeste has been very cooperative, Kelvin," he says. "She's remorseful about her role in the situation, and I know she will strive to be obedient in the future. I've accepted her apology."

Daddy glances from me to Mr. Nielsson. I also glance at Mr. Nielsson's sad face, and my heart aches for him. I wonder if Jon considered what his actions would do to his family. Maybe he knew better than to think about it.

That was my mistake.

THE WEEK DRAGS on. I find it harder and harder to get myself out of bed each morning. Every movement becomes an effort, as if the air is water and I have to push my body through it. My legs are dead weight and I feel like I'm sinking. Thoughts of Jon are with me every minute of every day, but instead of bringing me pleasure as they once did, now they only bring me pain. I miss him more than I thought possible.

Two evenings in a row the Prophet stopped by to visit Daddy. I saw him going into the barn and coming out about an hour later. When Daddy came into the house last night, he glanced at me. I couldn't read the expression on his face, but there was something different there. He knows something.

The Prophet has returned again this afternoon, but this time Martin Nielsson is with him. Daddy glances at me as he steps out the door. Does this have something to do with Jon? For the next half hour, my heart skitters around in my chest, wondering what they could be discussing. Mr. Nielsson's presence in our barn hasn't escaped Nanette's attention either. She volunteered to pull weeds in the garden, a chore she usually despises. I watch as she glances at the barn, hoping, I suppose, to force some kind of encounter with him.

This is not her lucky day. Daddy steps out of the barn, completely ignoring Nanette, and strides across the yard to the house. My stomach contracts and I feel a sudden and overwhelming need to relieve myself, but before I can, Daddy has reached the house and is ordering me to join him in his office. The last barn episode is still fresh in my mind as I force myself to follow behind him, but my legs are heavier than ever and each step is a huge effort. The sense of dread is overwhelming.

Nanette and I make eye contact as I pass. Her eyebrows arch, but I can only shrug and continue on to the barn.

As I step into the office, the Prophet and Mr. Nielsson get to their feet. I feel Jon's father studying me, and when I meet his eyes, he smiles a little. His face is sad, but the smile is kind. I decide I'm not in any new trouble.

The Prophet clears his throat. "Celeste, I have received direction from the Heavenly Father. Your assignment for marriage has been determined."

Now my heart, which had been beating erratically, begins to pound with a hard and steady beat. If I hadn't been so overwhelmed with grief these past few nights, I might have guessed at the reason for the Prophet's visits. Daddy no doubt asked the Prophet to hurry my assignment after the incident with Jon, but why is Mr. Nielsson here?

I glance at him, he cocks his head and the final puzzle piece slides into place. I feel all the blood rush from my head. The room goes black and starry, and I feel hands guiding me into a chair. When my vision returns, I look up to see all three men staring down at me.

"Celeste," Mr. Nielsson says. He's wringing his clasped hands. "I am most pleased to accept you as my celestial wife. It will be my honor to welcome you into my family."

I'm numb.

"Celeste," Daddy says. "Where are your manners?"

I open my mouth to speak, but there are no words. I simply shrug. I feel his eagle eyes on me.

"The marriage will take place this Sunday," the Prophet says.

My head jerks up to stare at him. It's unheard of for a marriage to take place so quickly. We should be given time to become acquainted.

"It will be a brief private ceremony," Daddy says. "Considering the trouble you've been in, we feel we should simply get it over with."

I am still too numb to respond. The room is quiet. Finally Mr. Nielsson speaks. "Sir," he says, addressing the Prophet, "I seek permission to speak with Celeste, alone."

The Prophet nods. Daddy sighs deeply, and the two of them leave the room. I hear the door of the barn bang shut.

Mr. Nielsson pulls a chair up so he's facing me. He reaches out and takes both of my limp hands in his. "Celeste," he says. "I know you're troubled. I miss Jon too. But I promise to take good care of you and our children. I pray you will learn to love me, as you do my son."

I do not trust myself to say anything and continue to stare at my lap.

"I am a gentle caring husband. I will never hurt you. My wives are good-hearted too. I believe you should count your blessings. Not all girls are so fortunate."

Perhaps I'm dreaming. This is just too unreal. Any minute now, I will wake from this nightmare, yet the gigantic lump in my throat feels all too real, and it threatens to suffocate me.

"Let us pray together, Celeste," he says.

I bow my head further. It's something that I can do.

"Our Father, we give thanks for your direction in these matters. We are truly blessed. As your humble servants, we will continue to aspire to the highest degree of celestial glory. It is the ultimate privilege to be married under laws which honor the sacred principle of plural marriage. Amen."

There's a pause, and I know he is waiting for me to say amen as well, but I am still without a voice.

"Would you care to walk with me, Celeste?"

I shake my head.

"You know, Celeste, there are two ways you can go with this." For the first time I detect a note of irritation in his voice. He lets go of my hands. "You can make it hard on yourself, or easy. Either way, the decision is made. You will be my wife. I suggest you go home and decide to be grateful, even joyous." He pauses and then adds, "The Prophet had considered taking you for his own wife. That might not have been so pleasant for you."

Now my head snaps up. He nods. "But your father thought it would be more fitting if you were assigned to me."

A surge of anger instantly dissolves the lump in my throat. "But God decides who girls are assigned to!"

Mr. Nielsson looks away. "For the most part He does, but sometimes it's a little unclear and the wisdom of the elders is required to sort it out."

I think about that. "Daddy thought it more *fitting* that I be married to you? So who is being punished here? You or me?"

"Why would I be punished, Celeste? I have done nothing wrong. And besides, I know you will make a lovely wife. This is God's will."

"Unless the Prophet misunderstood God's will."

He shrugs. "As I said, I think you need to count your blessings. Life would be much harder for you if you were married to the Prophet."

"Perhaps this is the Prophet's way of punishing Jon," I suggest. "Marrying me to his father."

Mr. Nielsson frowns. "I was warned that you had a vivid imagination, Celeste. And a rebellious streak."

Now I look away.

"You are fifteen," he continues, somewhat gruffly. "Your behavior with Jon reminds us that you are more than ready to become a wife. Despite your behavior, I am willing to take you."

I'm seeing a different side of this man. "The other day you told me you understood about being attracted to someone you are not assigned to."

"Indeed I did. What I was saying is that I know it happens. Acting on it is entirely different."

Who is this man? One moment he seems gentle and understanding, and the next he's as rigid as the Prophet.

"If you do not care to walk with me," he says, getting up, "I guess I won't see you until the ceremony. However, I welcome the opportunity to become better acquainted before then, so if you have a change of heart, have someone send me a message."

He turns to leave the room but swings around and regards me. Then he returns to stand in front of me. He leans over, takes my hands again and pulls me to my feet. The closeness between us makes me uncomfortable, and I take a step back. He takes a step forward and grips my shoulders with his hands. I try to step back again, but he holds me firm. Then he leans forward and presses his dry cracked lips onto mine. I feel nothing but revulsion and push him away. "We're not married yet," I tell him.

He sighs. "You may be disappointed that I am not my son," he tells me, "but I, too, am disappointed. I would've preferred to have your sister as my wife."

He turns and walks across the office but pauses at the door. "And between now and Sunday," he says, turning to me, "it would be wise for you to take the lead from her and practice purity."

And then he's gone.

❦ *Chapter Sixteen* ❦

$\mathcal{N}anette$

I can feel the burning heat of the sun right through my dress, but I won't go inside until I see Martin Nielsson come out of the barn. Daddy and the Prophet left a few minutes ago, but Celeste is still in there with him. What are they doing?

I know I did the right thing when I told Daddy about Celeste and Jon, but I admit I didn't consider what it would do to Mr. Nielsson's family. I should have known that Jon would leave Unity. He couldn't have stayed under the circumstances, but I heard Daddy's wives talking about the terrible sadness it brought to his family. I didn't mean to hurt them. It has also made Daddy permanently grouchy, and Celeste is more miserable now than ever. I've had a few moments of regret.

I lean back over the sprouting carrots and continue thinning the rows. The image of Celeste with Jon keeps replaying in my mind. Their bodies were pressed so close together, and their kiss was…I have no words for it. It was like…like they were desperate for each other. Something stirred inside me when I saw them. At first I thought it was just shock and anger at their disobedience, but now I wonder if it was something else. My own daydreams with Martin Nielsson have changed, and now I have us kissing like that, but only after we are married, of course.

I stand up when I hear the creak of the barn door. It's Mr. Nielsson and he's alone! He looks preoccupied, and he's staring at the ground as he walks, but he's heading this way. I quickly straighten my apron and wipe the sweat off my forehead with my handkerchief. He pushes the back gate open.

"Hello, Mr. Nielsson."

He looks up, startled.

"Oh, hello, Nanette," he says. His cheeks redden. Why is he blushing? "You're working in the garden, are you?"

"Yes."

His eyes dart nervously around the yard. "I've just been…talking. With Celeste," he says.

"Oh."

He nods his head. "Are you keeping well?"

"Yes, and you?"

He sighs heavily. "My son Jon left Unity. I'm sure you heard. It has torn a huge hole in my heart."

"Oh. I'm sorry."

He just stands there, rocking from one foot to the other.

"Is that why you were speaking with Celeste?"

"Huh? Oh. No." He's blushing again.

I wait, expecting him to explain.

"You may have seen the Prophet here too," he says.

"Yes. He was with Daddy."

"Yes, well, he was here to talk to Celeste as well."

"Oh."

"But I suppose I should not be discussing this with you. I will let your father explain. I have a few more things I wish to discuss with him. Is he here?"

"Yes, he's still with the Prophet, inside. You should go around to the front of the house and someone will let you in."

"Thank you, Nanette." He begins to walk away but swings around once more. "You are a lovely girl."

My face burns, but not from the sun. What do I say to that? You're a lovely man? No. I simply say, "Thank you." He smiles a little, nods and then walks off.

I gather up my gardening tools. It was worth working in the blistering sun. Now I know for sure that Mr. Nielsson feels the same about me as I do about him. God will see it too and direct the Prophet to assign me to him. I know it. I have been good and obedient. I have practiced purity. My efforts will be rewarded. It will truly be a match made in heaven. But how will I ever wait another year?

The barn door creaks open once more, and now I see Celeste coming toward the garden. Her shoulders are slumped, and she also stares at the ground as she walks, but then she always walks like that.

"Hi, Celeste," I say. She looks up, and I can see that she's been crying. I wonder how long it will take her to get over Jon. There's really no point in moping about like she's been doing. It's not going to make him come back.

She doesn't answer. She's been treating me like I'm invisible, and suddenly I don't feel like taking it anymore.

"I think it's time you forgot about him," I tell her as she walks past.

She swings around and glares at me. And then the expression on her face changes. She stands up a little straighter. "I've been assigned," she says.

"You have? To who?"

She doesn't answer but regards me curiously.

And then I understand. "No!" I say.

She just nods.

Anger surges through me, and I push her, hard. "He's waiting for me! I know he is!"

She pushes me back. "Apparently that's not the way God sees it."

"There's been a mistake," I tell her, the anger turning to panic. "I'll tell Daddy to talk to the Prophet. Maybe it's not too late to change things."

"Works for me," she says. "It's not like *I* want to marry *him*."

"It's not fair!" I shout. "I've been obedient and faithful, and you haven't."

Celeste turns and walks toward the house.

"What are you going to do?" I call to her back.

"About what?" she says.

"About getting married."

"What choice do I have?"

"You can say no."

Celeste stops and turns to look at me. "What are you saying, Nanette?"

"Tell him you won't marry him."

"And then what?"

"I don't know. But you don't want to get married. You always said that."

Celeste stares at me. "I'm surprised at you, Nanette. You're telling me to be disobedient."

I know I'm not making any sense, but the panic is making me crazy. "You've been disobedient before. Why not now, when it really counts?"

She takes a step closer to me. I'm feeling faint, maybe from the sun. "Even if I did refuse to marry him," she says, "even if I chose to disgrace my family and Mr. Nielsson, it still wouldn't mean that you would be assigned to him."

I know that what she's saying is true. But still, I can't bear to know that she is with him and I'm not.

"You could leave Unity," I tell her, shocking even myself. "Go find Taviana, and Jon."

Celeste is watching me, a curious expression on her face. "So you're no longer worried that I won't achieve eternal life," she says. "Or that I'll burn in hell. What happened to pure, obedient, caring Nanette?" She shakes her head. "It seems that even those who practice purity have their limit."

"Celeste," I say, "I'm sorry I told Daddy about you and Jon. But please, for me, don't marry Mr. Nielsson." Streams of sweat are running down my back and chest, and I'm beginning to see stars in the air between us. I have to get out of the sun.

She shrugs. "Who knows? Maybe we'll be sister wives as well as sisters in a couple of years." She shakes her head and continues her trudge toward the house.

My world goes black.

Chapter Seventeen

CELESTE

I run into the house and call for Daddy, and he and Mr. Nielsson carry Nanette into the living room and lay her on a sofa. She quickly regains consciousness.

"Bring a glass of water!" Mr. Nielsson snaps at me. I hand it to him and then watch as he leans over and gently puts it to her lips. I would have expected him to step aside and let one of Daddy's wives care for her, but he takes over. Nanette is right. It should be her marrying him and not me.

I slip out of the room and up the stairs to check on Mother. I'm shocked when I see her. She's lying on her side, her wet hair plastered to her head. All the blankets have been tossed to the floor and the window is wide open but it still feels like an oven in her room. Her dress has worked its way up her legs, and I can see that her ankles are grossly swollen. Her eyes are closed, her face deathly white, and she appears to be panting. I run back down the stairs and gather up another glass of water and a bowl and towel.

Back in her room, I wipe her face with cool water and push the hair away from her face. Her eyes flutter open, but she doesn't appear to recognize me for a moment.

"Mother, are you all right?"

"Celeste." Her eyes focus and she tries to sit up, but it requires too much effort. "I'm so warm."

I can feel waves of heat radiating from her body, and she smells like she hasn't been given a sponge bath in days.

"I brought you some water." I hold the glass to her lips, just as Mr. Nielsson did for Nanette a few minutes ago.

She drinks thirstily from the glass, and I go into the bathroom and fill it up again. When she's finished the second glass, she's ready to sit up. I fluff her pillows and make her comfortable. Now I see that her hands are also very swollen.

"It's warm for May, isn't it?" she says as I wipe her face with the wet towel.

"It is. Nanette just fainted from the heat."

"Is she all right?" she asks, frowning.

"I think she'll be fine. Mr. Nielsson is with her."

Mother's eyes widen. "Mr. Nielsson?"

"He was here talking to Daddy."

"Oh." I see understanding flicker across her face. Her hand moves to her enormous belly, and she rubs it. Then she reaches for my hand and places it near the top of the bulge. "This is an active one," she says. "Can you feel that kicking?"

Something sharp jabs me right through Mother's clothes. I pull my hand away, appalled. She doesn't seem to notice my reaction.

"There's nothing wrong with this little guy," she says, rubbing her stomach again.

I scan my mother's swollen body. Between pregnancies she's a tiny woman, but there's nothing small about her right now. I don't ever want to look like that. Some color has returned to her cheeks. "Are you going to be okay?"

"I think so," she says. She holds up a hand and regards it. "Though the swelling has me a little concerned. I don't remember puffing up like this before. It's probably just the heat."

I think about Colleen and how pale Mother looked when I first checked in on her. "Maybe we should tell Daddy to bring a doctor from Springdale to check you over," I suggest.

"I feel like I'd be a huge disappointment to your father if I can't manage this without help from the outside," she says, her voice hardly more than a whisper. "You know how he feels about our being independent. No one else has ever had to have a doctor."

By "no one else" she means Deborah and Lena.

"I know," I tell her, though I'm tempted to point out that Colleen might still be alive if her husband had consulted a doctor sooner. "But you've given him seven healthy children without help from the outside. Just this once, I think it would be good to get a doctor's opinion."

"Could you talk to him about it, Celeste? I don't want him to think I've lost faith."

"He's not exactly happy with me right now," I tell her. "But maybe I'll ask Nanette to talk to him. He always listens to her."

She nods. "Did he…talk to you about anything else today?"

I hear myself exhaling. "Yes. I've been assigned to Mr. Nielsson."

"He's a lovely man," she says. "I'm so happy for you." I see tears in her eyes.

I just shrug.

"He will treat you well. His wives are all happy."

"Nanette wishes she could be assigned to him."

"Maybe she will be too."

"I told her that. It didn't make her feel any better."

Mother's eyes widen, but she doesn't comment. She sinks deeper into her pillows. A breeze coming through the window lifts the filmy curtains. "Ahh, that's better," she says, fanning herself with her hand.

"I'll bring you some supper in a little while."

"Thank you, Celeste." She closes her eyes. "And you'll talk to Nanette, won't you? About talking to your father?"

"I will." I kiss her forehead and leave the room.

I find Nanette still stretched out on the sofa, but Mr. Nielsson is gone. "I just spoke with Mother," I tell her.

She regards me but doesn't say anything.

"We're both worried about the swelling in her hands and feet. She's wondering if you could tell Daddy that she should be looked at by a doctor from Springdale."

She struggles to a sitting position, frowning. "Talk to him yourself."

"We both feel that you might have more influence with him."

"I doubt that."

"Why do you say that?"

She looks over her shoulder to see who might be listening, but there are only small children in the room. "I asked him to tell the Prophet that I'm ready to be assigned to a husband, but he didn't do that."

"Maybe because you're too young."

"I might not be fifteen, but I'm ready."

"Well, I'm worried about Mother, and she's concerned about herself too. So if you care at all about her, I think you should go talk to Daddy right now. Think about what happened to Colleen."

She nods and slowly gets to her feet.

"Are you all right?"

"Yeah, just a little dizzy."

"Do you think you'll pass out again?"

She shakes her head and walks across the room. She pauses at the door, takes a deep breath and leaves the house.

Standing at the kitchen sink, I watch her cross the yard to the barn. I'm sure Daddy will listen to her when it comes to our mother. I know he's not supposed to have a favorite wife, but I think Mother is it anyway. And Nanette's clearly his favorite daughter, but then everyone has a soft spot for her. Except me.

I think about her pleas for me to refuse to marry Mr. Nielsson. That is so unlike her. It's amazing how love can make us do things we never dreamed we'd do. Two months ago I would not have believed that I'd break so many rules to see Jon. I'm sure Nanette is shocked at herself for suggesting that I continue to be disobedient.

I scrape potatoes and consider what she said. What if I did refuse to get married? Is it possible? I picture Daddy's face as I tell him that I won't be marrying Mr. Nielsson. After recovering from his shock he'd fly into a rage and reach for the leather strap. But I can outrun him. I don't need to consent to his demands. I feel myself smiling at the notion of outrunning him. But then what? Could I continue living here? No. A sense of doom settles over me again. It would bring too much shame on my family. Father would order me to leave. I would have to go to Springdale. I'd become an apostate, and I could never return to Unity.

I picture my last trip to Springdale, with my father, and I cringe when I remember how everyone was dressed, or not dressed, out on the streets, showing all their skin and letting their underwear hang out. It's one thing to let my ankles show on a deserted beach, quite another to be half naked in public. I could never be one of them.

I fill a pot with cold water. But Taviana came to Unity and adapted to us. And Jon is there. He would stick with me. I would not be alone.

I shake my head as I rinse the potatoes and put them in the water. I feel a lone tear trickling down my cheek. It is different for them. I can never leave. I might as well stop thinking about it.

In just a few days I will be part of Mr. Nielsson's family. This will no longer be my home. It's so hard to believe. When I marry him, I will become Jon's stepmother.

My children will be his stepsisters and brothers. We will be related, through marriage. The thought brings me no comfort as Jon will never return anyway.

I see Daddy coming back to the house with Nanette. Good. I knew he'd listen to her. They come in through the back door, and both of them climb the steps to Mother's room.

Fat from the frying pan spatters me as I drop a ground-beef patty into the pan. I hear Daddy's heavy footsteps coming back down the stairs. He bangs out the door, and a moment later the truck revs into life and pulls out of the driveway.

Nanette comes into the kitchen. "He's gone to get a doctor," she whispers.

I notice she's still pale. "Are you okay?" I ask her.

She nods. "But you're right. Mother looks awful. She wasn't nearly so bad when I brought her breakfast."

"She thinks maybe it's just the heat."

"Maybe." Nanette begins to wash vegetables, and together, in silence, we finish preparing supper.

Lena has just said the evening blessing when we hear Daddy's truck pulling back into the driveway. It is followed by another car. Nanette leaps to her feet and peers out the window. "He's brought a doctor," she says.

The front door swings open and Father comes into the house, the doctor trailing behind. "Deborah," he says from the kitchen door. "Please take Dr. Metcalf to Irene's room and remain there while he speaks with her."

Deborah nods and leads the man upstairs. Daddy takes his seat at the table, and I bring him a plate of food.

With the exception of babbling from the children, the table is quiet throughout the meal. I help little Joan with her supper, and Nanette assists Faith. Deborah and the doctor are still upstairs when family members begin excusing themselves from the table, so Pam and I start cleaning up dishes while Lena and Nanette herd the children outside for a final romp before their bedtime. The longer Deborah and the doctor are gone, the more knots develop in my stomach. Father waits at the table, preoccupied. I expect it was hard for him to swallow his pride and ask for assistance from a doctor. I hope Mother isn't too disappointed in herself.

We're almost finished in the kitchen, and I'm wondering how I can slip upstairs to Mother's room without Daddy noticing, when Deborah and the doctor come back down the stairs.

"I'd like to speak to you privately," the doctor says to my father. He glances about the kitchen, but his expression doesn't give anything away.

Daddy nods and leads the doctor a short way down the driveway where they can talk alone.

"Well?" I ask Deborah.

She's taking her plate of food out of the oven where I've put it to keep warm. "He says she needs to be in a hospital. Her blood pressure is too high, and the swelling is not good."

"Do you think Daddy will listen?"

She shrugs. "I don't know. But maybe, because of Colleen."

"Could she die if she doesn't get help?" Nanette asks, her eyes wide.

"I don't know. But the doctor did ask why she didn't seek medical attention sooner."

"Then Daddy better take her to the hospital." Nanette's voice quivers.

Through the window, I watch the two men in the driveway. The conversation seems to be going back and forth, and then I see the doctor put his finger to Daddy's chest and poke him aggressively a few times. Daddy takes a step back, and the doctor straightens his shoulders and returns to his car. "He's leaving," I tell the others.

A moment later, Daddy is back in the house. He stands in the kitchen doorway, not saying anything. Finally he comes to a decision. "Deborah, go tell Lena to pack a bag for Irene. She'll come with me when I take Irene to the hospital."

"What is it, Daddy?" Nanette asks, jumping to her feet. "Is she going to be okay?"

Daddy ignores her. "And Deborah, you're in charge here until we return. I don't know when that will be."

My own heart feels lodged in my throat. Without asking permission, I slide past him and scramble up the stairs to Mother's room. I hear Nanette on the stairs behind me.

Mother looks exactly as I left her. "Daddy's taking you to the hospital," I tell her.

"He is?" Her room is somewhat cooler than it was this afternoon, but her hair is still wet with perspiration, and her skin is deathly white. The empty glass stands on her night table. I grab it and dash into the bathroom to fill it up.

When I reenter her room, Nanette is sitting on the bed beside her, stroking her huge belly. I help Mother sip from the glass of water. "Should I go get you some dinner before you go?" I ask her.

"No, but thank you, Celeste, and you too, Nanette, for your help. I feel relieved to be going to a hospital, even though it bends the rules of our faith."

I picture the way the doctor was poking my father in the chest and wonder how close Daddy came to making a different decision.

"Will you stay there until the baby is born?" I ask her.

"I believe so," she tells me. "But I trust you girls to take care of your little brothers and sisters for me."

"We will," Nanette assures her.

I think of telling her that I'll be married in a couple of days, and once I'm married I'll be living at the Nielssons' farm, but decide against it. She has enough to worry about right now, and perhaps this will give me the leverage I need to have the whole thing postponed.

Lena comes into the room, smiles at Mother and puts a fresh nightdress and housecoat into a small bag.

"I think they give you hospital gowns to wear there," Mother says.

"Oh, but they're not modest. You'll feel much more comfortable in your own things."

Mother just nods. "Girls, could you help me get dressed for the trip to Springdale?"

She is very shaky on her feet, but once she is dressed, she puts an arm around each of our shoulders and we help her down the stairs. Daddy has collected the rest of her children in the living room. We settle her into the armchair and gather around her. We hand her Faith and Joan, one at a time, for a little cuddle. Rebecca and the boys are shy around her. It's been a while since she's been involved in their lives.

"I'm going away for a few days," she tells the boys and Rebecca, "because I need some extra help with this baby." She rubs her belly. "But I'll be back soon. I know you'll be good while I'm gone. I'll miss all of you."

"How long?" Rebecca asks. She leans against Mother's legs. I know she longs to be in Mother's lap too, but with the unborn baby and Faith already there, there is no room. I bend over and pick her up.

"Not too long," Mother says. "It's almost time for the baby to be born."

"I don't want you to go," Rebecca whines, and her face crumples as tears stream down her cheeks.

I hug her to me, but she pushes me away and wiggles to be put down. She runs back to Mother's legs and hangs on for dear life.

"We'd best be going," Daddy says. He and Lena bend over to help Mother out of her chair, but Rebecca won't let go of her leg. She's wailing, which starts the babies crying too. My little brothers just stand back, watching, but their faces are long. "Take this child away," Daddy barks at me. I pull Rebecca away, astonished at how strong she is. I wrap my arms around her thrashing body and sink into the armchair with her as Lena and Daddy help Mother out the door. Mother glances back once, but Daddy pulls her forward. Deborah has come into the room to help Nanette with the twins, and Rebecca quits struggling but sobs into my chest. One by one, she is losing her family. First Taviana. Now Mother. How will she feel when I too leave the day after tomorrow? I keep holding her until she cries herself to sleep.

DADDY AND LENA returned to Unity late last night. The hospital wouldn't let them stay with Mother all night, and having no other place to go, they came home.

The house has been quiet today. Nobody has the energy for bickering. We go about our chores and quietly pray for Mother.

I'm putting clean sheets on the beds in the girls' room when Deborah finds me. She stands in the doorway and watches for a moment. I simply ignore her.

"I understand you've been assigned to Mr. Nielsson," she says.

I nod and shake a clean sheet over a mattress.

"That's very exciting," she says, joining me at the bed. "Mr. Nielsson is known to be a kind and caring husband." She tucks in the sheet and helps me straighten blankets.

"That's what he told me."

"You could do a lot worse," she says.

"He told me that too."

"You don't sound very happy," she says.

I don't bother answering. She knows why I'm being rushed into marriage.

"Your father asked me to find you something to wear on Sunday," she says. "Would you like to see it?"

I simply shrug.

"I know your mother will wish she were here, but I guess that's not possible."

"You don't think Daddy would consider postponing the ceremony until the baby's been born?"

"Apparently not. He asked me to help you get ready for Sunday."

"What else are you supposed to do?"

"Well," she says, sitting down on one of the beds. "I'm supposed to talk to you about husband-wife relations."

I feel my face burn. "I know about them."

"You do?" Her eyes widen.

"Girls talk. I've heard."

"Oh." She looks so relieved I almost laugh. "Well then, I'll bring you the dress later. Let me know if it needs any altering. I don't think it should. It's the same one Pam wore when she married your father, and you look close to the same size. Is there anything else I can do to help you prepare?"

Deborah and I have never gotten along very well, but suddenly I realize that she might be my best hope for delaying my imminent marriage. I sit beside her on the bed. "Deborah, I'm so worried about Mother," I tell her honestly. "I'm not in a good state of mind to get married. I admit,

I'm not keen on getting married at all, but if I have to, I want it to be as perfect as I can make it." That part's not quite so honest. "Do you think there's any way you can convince Daddy to delay it for me? I really think it's only fair to Mr. Nielsson."

She regards me. Then she puts her arm awkwardly around my shoulders. "I'll see what I can do, Celeste. I agree, and it's not really fair for your mother to have her eldest daughter married while she is away like this. I'd want to be there for my daughter."

"Thanks, Deborah. I knew you'd understand."

Actually, I didn't expect that at all, but she is a mother of daughters too, so I should have realized she might see it from that point of view.

DEBORAH LOOKS AT me across the kitchen table at breakfast. She shakes her head and frowns. Then her eyes drop to her plate. I feel the blood drain from my head. Has something happened to Mother?

Daddy turns to me. "I'm going into Springdale to see your mother this morning," he says. "Perhaps you'd like to come with me so she can give you her blessing for tomorrow's ceremony. Lena will also be coming, and we'll do the shopping while you're with Irene."

I don't know whether to laugh or cry. Deborah had only been telling me that she couldn't get the ceremony postponed. It wasn't bad news about Mother, which is a huge relief, but now I have no hope of postponing the ceremony. My heart sinks.

This is my last day, ever, of being just a girl. Tomorrow I will be a wife.

I nod at my father. "How soon are we leaving?"

Chapter Eighteen

Taviana

I watch Jon's face as he slides the salt and vinegar potato chip onto his tongue. His mouth puckers. "Yuck!" he says and passes the bag back to me.

I smile and continue eating them. It's been fun introducing him to junk food. Mostly he doesn't like it. I don't crave it much anymore either, but it's nice to have the odd treat.

We're at the park in town. I haven't found a job, or a place to live, and my days are running out fast.

"I still don't understand why you don't go back to school," he says. "We'd be there together, watching out for each other."

"Trust me, Jon. You'll be fine. I wouldn't be. I've tried it before."

I was so stoked to see Jon when Jimmy brought him to Abigail's house that I gave him a big hug. It was like seeing an old friend, even though I'd only met him once.

He'd agreed to all of Abigail's rules, and Jimmy was hoping to find him a job in construction for the summer. Abigail figured there was no sense starting school at this point in the spring, but she was going to meet with the school counselors to determine what grade he should start at in the fall. She also hoped to pick up some books for him to study over the summer to help him catch up. He hadn't been in school since he was fourteen.

For the first couple of days he seemed delighted to be at Abigail's. He knew Selig and Matthew and had met Jimmy when Jimmy visited Unity. Abigail showered him with attention. She seemed more comfortable around the boys than she did around me. Jon was amazed by TV and was happy to watch it all day.

He'd been mopier the last couple of days. I suspect the overwhelming truth of what he'd done had sunk in, and he was probably feeling miserable about hurting his family. He would be missing Celeste too, and his home. When he asked me what I thought her father would do to her, I could only shrug. A quick marriage was my best guess, but I didn't tell him that.

I brought him into town with me today to take his mind off things. "Let's go to the library," I suggest.

He nods and follows me out of the park. I push open the door and the librarian greets me. "Taviana, your card is ready."

"All right!" I go over to her desk and collect it from her. "Now I can read every single last book in this place," I say.

She laughs and wishes me luck. I introduce her to Jon. "Would you like to apply for a card too?" she asks him.

He looks to me for assistance. "Yes, he would," I tell her. "He's new to libraries, but I know he's going to love them as much as I do."

He smiles and nods at the woman.

She pushes the form across the counter to him. "Just fill it in," she tells him, "and we'll make you a card, and then you'll be free to read every single last one of the books in this place too."

Jon's eyebrows arch as he looks around. "Okay," he says, sounding uncertain.

The librarian and I laugh. "I'll give him a tour," I tell her.

I show him how the books are separated into categories, as well as fiction and non-fiction. He asks if there are books on cars. I lead him to the right section and leave him there while I browse through the novels. Then I show him the computers. I sit him down at one and attempt to explain how the Internet works. I ask him what he wants to learn about. He thinks for a moment and says, "Inuksuk." That throws me for a moment, but then I remember Celeste telling me that they were building them together on the beach. I type in the word *inuksuk*, and we watch as a list of sites appear. I show him how to point the cursor at the first site and right-click on the mouse.

A moment later a page appears with photos of all different kinds of inuksuk. I show him how to scroll down to find more information.

"Look at them all," he says. He looks up at me, standing beside him, a big smile on his face. "This is amazing!" The smile turns sad. "I wish I could show this to Celeste."

I nod. "You can find a lot of cool stuff on the Internet," I tell him.

"Are there books on inuksuk too?" he asks

We go to the library catalog, and I show him how to look for them. Then we find our way to the rack where the books on the Inuit culture are shelved. He pulls one after another off the rack. "I'd sure like to read these," he says.

"Choose two," I tell him, "and I'll take them out on my card. When you get your own card, you can take out as many as you want."

Back at the front desk, I pass the librarian the stack of books I plan to borrow with my new card. As she's signing them out for me, she asks if I know of any students who are looking for summer employment.

"Doing what kind of work?" I ask, trying to remain calm.

"Mostly shelving returned material," she says. "To cover for our staff who take summer holidays. But we also have a summer reading club for children, and we need some enthusiastic people to help run that program as well. It would include reading stories to our youngest patrons."

Jon and I look at each other. "Well, go on," he says.

"How do I apply?" I ask the librarian.

"You're looking for work?" she asks.

I nod.

"Well, that's wonderful! I was secretly hoping you were when I asked. You seem like the kind of girl who would like working in a library."

"How did you figure that out?" I laugh, glancing at my stack of books.

She steps into her office and brings back a job application form.

"Can I fill this in right now?" I ask.

"Sure." She hands me a pen. "You can sit at one of those tables." She motions to an area where people are working.

Jon sits across from me, filling in his library card application. When we're finished, we turn in both forms.

"I will put in a good word for you," she tells me and winks.

"Thank you! I'd love to shelve books and work with children. It sounds like a perfect job."

"We'll call you when we start interviewing, which should be the middle of next week."

"Oh."

"Is something the matter?"

"No, not really. I'd just hoped to hear sooner than that."

"We have to go through the proper procedure. But I'm sure you have a very good chance at the job."

"Thanks. I hope so."

Outside the library, I slump onto a bench. "I have to leave Abigail's in a couple of days. She gave me one week to stay with her, so I won't be at the phone number I put on my application."

"Maybe she'll give you an extension."

"Maybe." But I know her reputation for sticking with the rules.

WHILE WE'RE WAITING for the bus, I see someone with a long dress walking into the hardware store across the street. Someone from Unity. It has to be one of Kelvin's wives on their weekend shopping expedition.

"I just thought of something I need," I tell Jon. "Wait here. I'll be right back." I jog across the street and slip into the store. Sure enough, there's Kelvin in the automotive section. He's discussing something with the salesperson. I see Lena browsing in the gardening area.

"Lena," I whisper, hiding behind a display of rakes.

She hears me and looks up. Her mouth drops open when she sees me. I move into the lighting aisle, hidden from the automotive section. Lena follows me.

"How is everyone?" I ask her.

"Irene's not good," she whispers. "She's in the hospital here. Celeste is with her."

"What's wrong?"

"High blood pressure, swollen hands and feet." She peers around to see if Kelvin can hear our conversation.

"How about Celeste? What happened to her after Jon left?"

She checks over her shoulder again. "She's getting married tomorrow. To Martin Nielsson."

"Martin Nielsson? Jon's father?"

Lena nods.

I can't believe it. Now that I'm once again on the outside, the traditions of The Movement seem much stranger.

"How are you?" Lena asks me.

"I'm surviving. But I miss all of you."

Lena smiles gently. Then her eyes narrow. "Kelvin and I will be here for a while yet. Why don't you go see Celeste and Irene at the hospital?"

My heart leaps. "I will. Right now. Thanks, Lena."

She slides out of the lighting aisle and continues browsing in the gardening area.

I race across the street to where Jon is sitting with our stack of books. "Celeste is at the hospital right now!" I tell him, out of breath.

He sits up. "What's the matter?"

"It's her mother. She's there visiting."

"Oh." He stares at me, not quite comprehending.

"We can go over there right now," I tell him. "You can see her."

Now his eyes widen. He grabs the bag with all the books. "Which way?"

We jog down the street and round the corner. We can see the hospital at the end of the block. "I will go up and see them," I tell Jon. "And then I'll try to talk to Celeste alone. I'll tell her you're waiting in the front lobby. When she finds you, the two of you need to get out of the lobby as fast as you can so that when her father returns, he won't see you."

"Where will we go?"

"I'm sure you'll figure something out."

He nods.

"And Jon, there's something else you need to know."

"Yeah?"

"Celeste is getting married. Tomorrow."

His eyes widen. "She is?"

I nod and take a deep breath. "To your father." I exhale heavily.

He just stares at me, and then he turns completely around so his back is to me. His hands go to his face.

I put my hand on his back. "Are you going to be okay?"

His head bobs, but he doesn't turn around.

"We don't have much time, so I'm going to go find them now."

His head bobs some more. I turn and walk down the street.

Chapter Nineteen

CELESTE

D addy and Lena have gone off to do the shopping, so I'm alone with Mother. The nurses have insisted that she wear the standard hospital gown, so she has a blanket pulled right up under her chin despite the heat in the room.

"You will adjust to your new family very quickly, I'm sure," Mother says, though I can see the look of concern in her eyes. One by one, her helpers are disappearing. First Taviana and now me, and it means a lot more work for the other wives. There have already been signs of resentment from Lena and Deborah, and the fact that Mother gets special attention from Daddy doesn't help matters.

"Perhaps Mr. Nielsson will allow me to return each day to help Nanette," I say. "Just until you are well again."

"Perhaps," she says. "Though it's usually best to cut the ties right away, to help you adjust to your new family."

"But it's different right now," I tell her. "It won't be for long. Didn't you say the doctors want to deliver your baby early?"

"That's what they said." She sighs. "But it all depends on whether your father will allow me to sign the consent papers. He's determined that I deliver this baby naturally."

"How do they want to deliver it?"

"By surgery. They think it should come out now and that labor might be too hard on me."

"Then just sign those consent papers!"

She sighs again. "I need his permission, but I think he'll come around."

I don't know whether she truly believes that or not. It was hard enough for Daddy to consent to her being in the hospital.

"But let's talk about you, Celeste. I am so disappointed that I won't be at the ceremony tomorrow. You'll let Deborah do your hair and help you get dressed?"

I shrug. "I can manage it myself."

I see Mother staring at someone behind me, so I turn around to see who is there. For a moment I don't recognize her. And then I'm on my feet and in her arms. "Taviana!"

When I finally let her go, there are tears streaming down both our cheeks. She turns to my mother. "Irene."

"Taviana." Mother's eyes are filled with tears too. "How did you know to find us here?"

Taviana sits on Mother's bed and picks up her hand. "I saw Lena in town. I was able to talk to her without Kelvin seeing us. I hope you don't mind."

"It is so wonderful to see you. How are you?"

She shrugs. "Not bad. I'm not living on the streets yet. And I just applied for a job working at the library."

"That's terrific!" my mother says, though I know she believes the library is stocked with books that fill people's heads with impure thoughts. I believed that not so long ago too. Now I'm not so sure. Taviana's stories always seemed harmless.

A nurse comes into the room and wraps a blood-pressure gage around Mother's arm. "Let's wait in the hall, Celeste," Taviana suggests.

I'm about to protest, but then I notice how intently she's looking at me. "Okay."

Taviana takes my arm, and we move a few steps down the hallway. "Jon is downstairs in the lobby," she whispers.

I can only stare at her, unbelieving.

"Go down and see him," she tells me. She pushes the button to call the elevator. "But you haven't got long. Your father will be back soon, so make sure you go somewhere so that he doesn't run right into you when he comes back."

"My mother..." I say.

"I'll stay with her," she says. "I'll say you're in the bathroom."

My blood is pounding in my head, and I can barely think. I push open the door to the stairwell and begin jogging down, not bothering to wait for the elevator, which I don't like anyway. When I reach the main floor, I push open the swinging door. Jon is standing right there, waiting. We stare at each other for a long awkward moment, and then I find myself in his arms. He hugs me hard. His breathing is ragged against my chest. I step back and look into his face. "Are you okay?"

He nods and wipes his nose with his sleeve. I pull a handkerchief out of my apron pocket and realize that it's the one he once lent me. I hand it to him. "It's yours," I tell him gently.

He takes it and tries to smile, but I notice his hand is shaking. "I'm sorry," he says. "I didn't want you to see me like this."

I glance about and notice the stares we're getting. Girls dressed like me aren't usually seen hugging young men. "Where should we go?"

Now Jon glances about too. He nods at a sign that says *Visitor's Waiting Area.* "That should work," he says.

The waiting room is empty, and Jon shuts the door behind us. He quickly gathers me into another hug. It feels incredible. I breathe him in, savoring the unexpected meeting. Tension melts away.

Eventually we let go of each other and sit side by side on the vinyl couch, facing each other, hands clasped. "I never thought I'd see you again," I tell him. "This is such a shock."

"I know," he says, squeezing my hands. "I've missed you so much." He leans forward and kisses me. I feel myself floating away.

The door bangs open. We jump apart, but it's just a woman with a small child. She sees us and decides not to stay.

"Celeste," Jon says, suddenly sitting up. His eyes shine. "Don't go back to Unity."

My entire body clenches from fear or excitement, I don't know which.

"Stay here with Taviana and me. We've found a nice lady who lets us live in her home as long as we go to school. You can come with us. We'll be together." Jon's clutching my hands, leaning into me.

I sit back, breathing hard. Should I do it? I could spend every day with them, going to school, just being together, no little children to mind, no mothers to boss me around. And I wouldn't have to marry Mr. Nielsson! A shudder runs through me when I remember his kiss, so different from the one Jon and I just shared. If I go back, I'll be sentenced to spend the rest of my life and all eternity with Mr. Nielsson. It's unbearable to think about.

And yet...running away would cause such pain in my family. I exhale, not realizing I've been holding my breath. I think of my mother, upstairs, lying in the hospital bed, so bloated and unwell. And Rebecca. I would never lay eyes on her again.

I get up and pace the waiting room. This is my opportunity to start a new life. My only opportunity. I do not have to be a wife and mother. I could have a career. Jon and Taviana are both managing. I have a choice.

I take another deep breath and exhale again. I can feel Jon staring at me, waiting for my answer. I know I have to make a decision right now. I look down at Jon, sweet sweet Jon, who is watching me, so hopefully.

But then I think of my father, and I close my eyes. I see the rage in his face, hear it in his voice. My resolve sinks just thinking about him.

I collapse on the couch beside Jon, and now I'm crying again. He passes me the handkerchief. We're back in each other's arms, rocking back and forth.

I'm aware of time passing, that Daddy will be finished his shopping and returning to the hospital, if he's not already here. I think of Mother, upstairs in her hospital bed, so sick that the doctors want to do surgery to remove the baby. I try to imagine never seeing her again, and I think of Rebecca and her sad little face when Mother left us the other night. But mostly I think of Daddy, and his fury. The shame of me running away would tear him apart, and in turn, he would make everyone miserable. I would be to blame. I pull myself away from Jon and shake my head.

He doesn't plead or beg. He simply clenches his teeth and his shoulders slump. He stares at his hands in his lap.

I stand up and walk to the door. I want to say goodbye, say something wise and meaningful, but nothing comes to mind.

"I love you, Jon."

It's the best I can do.

THE SIMPLE CEREMONY is not as simple as I'd imagined it to be. All of Mr. Nielsson's family is here, as well as all of mine, except Mother and the smallest babies.

Deborah has pulled my hair up with elastics and pins, and there are a few strands dangling around my face. The dress is long and white, and a little too snug, but I don't complain. I will only be wearing it for a few hours anyway.

At the altar, I stand facing Mr. Nielsson, and the Prophet stands facing the two of us. Across from him, with her back to our families, is Norah, Mr. Nielsson's first wife, who will be part of the service. Mr. Nielsson reaches over and takes my hands in his. He leans forward and whispers in my ear, "You look lovely, Celeste."

I don't meet his eyes or acknowledge what he has said. I am completely numb, hardly even aware that I am here. Ever since I left Jon at the hospital, I have felt an overwhelming sense of hopelessness.

The service begins. The Prophet drones on about the many children Mr. Nielsson's wives will bring him and how we are the jewels in his crown. I tune it all out and think of Jon and what it would be like if it were the two of us here, instead of me with his father.

The Prophet becomes silent, and I feel everyone's eyes on me. I look up. Mr. Nielsson tilts his head, waiting. I am supposed to say something but I don't know what.

The Prophet repeats himself. "Your father tells me that you feel you belong in Brother Martin's house."

I look at Daddy, standing behind Mr. Nielsson. His eyes bore into mine, and he's grinding his teeth. I have been taught the correct response, but my mind is blank. I open my mouth. Nothing.

Daddy clears his throat and looks even fiercer. I rack

my brain for the words I'm supposed to say. The Prophet repeats himself one more time. "Your father tells me that you feel you belong in Brother Martin's house, Celeste."

It's not too late. I could walk out the door, down the road, and never return. I could be in Jon's arms in just a few hours.

But Daddy's eyes won't let my feet move. I wonder, vaguely, how God feels when one of His children tells a lie in a place of worship. "I want to marry the one the Lord has revealed to be the one for me," I say, sinking into a pool of total emptiness.

Daddy's eyes close for a moment in relief. I'm sure he was as uncertain as I was that I'd go through with this.

Norah is instructed to place her hands on top of mine, a symbol of welcoming me into their family. Mr. Nielsson places his hands under mine. The final blessing is made, and then the Prophet says, "You may now kiss the bride."

I steel myself for the inevitable, and Mr. Nielsson leans forward and kisses me gently.

I am now Mrs. Nielsson. The sixth.

A SMALL CELEBRATION lunch with sandwiches and juice is held in the basement of the church. The wives mingle and the children run around playing tag. I see Nanette at her usual spot, pouring juice. Despite the fact that it is my marriage we're celebrating, I feel completely alone. Pam joins me at the side of the room.

"Are you okay?" she asks.

I shrug. "I guess."

"I…I know how you feel."

"You didn't want to marry my father?"

She shakes her head. "I was scared to death of him."

"And you still are?"

She nods. "Sort of."

"Me too." I think about how his eyes pinned me to the spot at the altar. I exhale deeply. Again.

"I saw Taviana yesterday," I tell her.

"You did?" Her eyes light up.

"I was in the hospital visiting my mother. She heard Mother was there, so she came up to see us."

"What about your father?"

"He was picking up supplies."

"How is she?"

"She seemed well. She said she was hoping to get a job at the library."

Pam thinks about that. "That makes sense. She always told great stories."

I smile, remembering.

"Did she ever tell you the one about Cinderella?" Pam asks.

I nod.

"That was always my favorite. I think about it when, well, you know."

"Yeah, I know." I look into her sad face and shrug. "But I don't think we're going to get rescued by a handsome prince."

We watch as a couple of little boys race past us. One of them is my brother, and the other one, I realize with a shock, is now my stepson.

"Are you worried about…later?" she whispers.

I look at her, surprised. "Not really worried," I admit. "Just dreading it."

"It's not so bad," she says. "And it really doesn't take so long."

I glance at her and see that she's blushing.

She shrugs. "Maybe it will be better for you. Some women say they love it."

I WON'T CLAIM to love it, but I suffered through it, and Martin, as I now have to call him, tried not to hurt me.

When we arrived at his house after the wedding, we had dinner with his family. I was treated like a guest and not permitted to help. I noticed the curious looks from his small children, but they all kept their distance, mostly studying me from behind their mothers' skirts. Four of Martin's wives greeted me warmly and introduced me to their children. Only one, Gail, kept her distance. One of his older boys, who is probably closest to Jon in age, actually winked at me when no one else was looking. I was shocked and quickly looked away.

I stabbed at the food on my plate but couldn't swallow anything. After the meal, Martin took my hand and led me down a long hallway until we reached a room that he said would be mine. He showed me other empty rooms along the way, rooms that he hoped would soon be filled with our children. This wing was a new addition to the house. Like my own father's home, this one was constantly being expanded as Martin's family grew. It resembled one of the motels along the highway near Springdale.

My room had only one bed and the walls were bare. There was a lamp on a bedside table, and someone had brought over the box that I'd packed my spare dress, nightdress and underclothes in, but that was it. The paint smelled fresh, and the room looked like it had never been occupied.

Closing the door behind us, Martin took me by the shoulders and turned me to face him. He cupped his hand under my chin and lifted my face to his. I wanted to close my eyes, shut him out, yet I didn't think this was a good time to make him angry. I stared at a mole above his right eyebrow, trying to hide the revulsion that he would surely read in my eyes.

He stroked my cheek with his thumb and told me he knew I didn't want to be with him, that he understood but hoped that soon I would grow to love him. His breath was sour, and I turned my face away. Then he began to undo the buttons on the front of my dress. I looked down at his hands and saw that they were trembling.

When it was over, I lay on my bed, naked and numb. Martin lay on his stomach beside me, an arm flung over my chest. I wondered if the rest of the family had heard his groaning or the squeaking of the bedsprings. I thought about the boy who'd winked and felt my face flush in embarrassment.

I rolled away, curling into a ball, my back to Martin. After a few minutes I heard him get up and felt a blanket settling over me. I refused to look at him. I could hear him dressing, and then I heard the door closing behind him. I'm guessing that he spent the rest of the night with someone who could show him affection in return. I felt myself shaking. I pulled the blanket up, conscious of the burning between my legs. The room was too quiet. I actually missed Nanette's warm body pressed up to mine, her soft breathing tickling my skin.

I had never felt so alone.

MY FIRST MORNING in the Nielsson kitchen is awkward. By the time I arrive, everyone is busy and there seems to be no place in the routine for me. At breakfast I'm careful not to meet the eyes of the boy who winked the night before, but I can feel his presence across the table and my face burns. I help with the dishes, but when they are done, I don't know what I should do next. All the chores seem to be taken care of. I find Norah nursing her youngest baby in the living room. She smiles kindly when I sit down beside her.

"Are you okay?" she asks gently.

I nod but feel my eyes burning. I blink to hold back the tears.

"He's a good man, Celeste. You'll get used to it."

Used to it? Is that the best I can hope for? I sigh, thinking of Jon and how I could be with him right now. "Is Gail Jon's mother?" I ask.

She nods but doesn't look at me. "It's not that she blames you," Norah says. "She knew Jon was restless, but she made it clear that it would be hard for her to have you in the family."

"She told everyone that?"

Norah nods. "She's very upset about Jon."

I sigh. It's not like I asked to be in the family. "So, what would you like me to do?" I ask.

"What would you like to do?"

"I'm good in the garden and the kitchen," I tell her. "I'm not as good with small children."

She smiles at me. "I like your honesty."

I think about that. "Well," I tell her, "if you want the whole truth, I'm really worried about how things are going in my father's home. With Mother in the hospital, Nanette will have her hands full with my little brothers and sisters. Daddy's other wives help out, of course, but they have their hands full too. I'm wondering how they're coping."

"Then why don't you go over there and see if they need you. I'm sure Martin would understand. He's out in the field with the boys right now, but at lunch we can check with him."

"Really? Thank you!"

I'm out the door before she can change her mind.

THE CONTRAST BETWEEN Martin's household and Daddy's hits me hard when I push open the door. I'd left an orderly cheerful atmosphere at Martin's, but here there are voices raised in anger and babies wailing from all corners of the house. The first person I see is Nanette, and she glares at me. "What are you doing here?"

"I came to see if you need some help."

"You don't live here anymore." She turns and begins to storm down the hall but nearly collides with Rebecca, who has come flying out of the kitchen. "Celeste!" she screams and races toward me, practically knocking me off my feet. I pick her up and hug her to my chest. Then I hold her out and look at her face. Her eyes are puffy from crying, and there are dark circles under her eyes.

I make eye contact with Nanette, who is watching us, arms folded across her chest.

"She's been crying nonstop since you left," Nanette says.

"I told you I'd come and visit," I tell Rebecca.

She just presses her face into my shoulder. I can feel her ragged breathing.

"If you really want to help, you can get her out of here for a while," Nanette says. She rolls her eyes. "She's setting everyone else off."

"Do you want to go for a walk, Becca?" I ask.

Her head nods against my shoulder.

"Okay," I tell Nanette. "But isn't there something else that you need help with? The babies?"

"I can handle them," she says.

"Is there any news?" I decide not to say the word *Mother* in front of Rebecca, but Nanette knows what I'm asking. She just shakes her head.

I place Rebecca on the floor. "Go get your shoes and a hat, then, and we'll go for a little walk, just you and me."

I watch as she races up the stairs. Nanette has turned her back to me, but she hasn't left the front hall. We listen to Lena and Deborah arguing over the misbehavior of one of Deborah's children in the kitchen. A moment later, Rebecca is scampering back down the stairs with a pair of shoes and her hat. I help her put them on.

"I don't have to be back at…" I am about to say Martin's but change my mind. "At Nielssons' until lunchtime, so if you think of anything else I can do to help, let me know."

"We're managing just fine without you," Nanette snaps, her back still turned to me.

I try to think of something to say. I suddenly feel sorry for her, and I'd like to rekindle our friendship, but the gulf between us feels so wide. "I'm sorry everything turned out this way, Nanette," I tell her. "It's not what I wanted either."

Her shoulders shrug, but she doesn't answer. Rebecca grabs my hand and starts pulling me toward the door. With a last look at Nanette's back, I step outside with Rebecca.

IT'S A BEAUTIFUL morning, there's a light breeze and the new leaves on the trees and shrubs still have the lushness of early spring. Rebecca and I walk hand in hand without talking. It's the first freedom I've tasted in days. I'm no longer a prisoner in my home. I should feel relaxed, but the constant ache of missing Jon plagues me, and the thought of spending the rest of my life and all eternity with Martin weighs heavily on my mind. Before yesterday there was always hope that something would change...that this would not be the way my life turned out. I had my chance to escape...but I didn't take it. I couldn't take it. Now there is nothing to look forward to, ever.

Rebecca leads the way, and soon I realize she's taking me to the playground near the river. Even though I have permission to be here, I still don't want Martin to see me, so we take the long way around to avoid walking past his fields.

At the playground, I push Rebecca on the swings, catch her as she slips down the slide and watch her hang on the monkey bars. Before long, the puffiness around her eyes disappears and her cheeks grow rosy again. Life is so much less complicated when you're four. Or five. Rebecca just had a birthday too. I sit on the bench and look out toward the river.

"Want to throw rocks in the water?" I ask her when she grows tired of the playground. She nods, taking my hand, and we stroll toward the water's edge. The ache of missing Jon intensifies here, the memories are so fresh, yet this place makes me feel closer to him at the same time.

When we reach the river, I glance upstream. The community of inuksuks appears to have grown. I wait until

Rebecca has tired of throwing stones before I take her hand and walk toward the stone people.

"What are those?" Rebecca asks as we approach.

"Inuksuks," I tell her. I notice that a couple of the balanced rock formations have also joined the community.

"What are they for?" she asks.

"They are just fun to make."

She wanders between them, and I wonder if she will push them over, the way she does with her block towers at home. She doesn't.

I study the new ones. Two more of them have been created to look like women. I find myself smiling.

Rebecca is studying the tower of balanced rocks. "Do you want to try making one of those?" I ask her.

She shakes her head. "Let's make an insuk," she says.

"Inuksuk," I correct her. "Sure. Shall we make one together, or do you want to make your own?"

"Together," she says.

We set to work, our skirts tucked into our aprons. By the time we're finished, three new inuksuks have joined the group. Two of them are children inuksuks, which was Rebecca's suggestion. We step back and admire our new creations. These inuksuks multiply almost as fast as the people of my community, I think to myself. The thought makes me smile.

I look down and find Rebecca staring up at me. "What?"

"You look nice when you smile."

I study her little face, which looks so much happier than it did when I collected her from home. Then I lean down and tickle her ribs. She shrieks and laughs. "So do you," I tell her.

$\mathcal{N}anette$

How can God have let me down like this? I have been obedient. I have practiced purity. And yet I feel I'm being punished.

Watching Celeste being wed to Martin Nielsson yesterday was hell on earth for me, and then last night I tossed and turned in my empty bed, imagining what they were doing together. I knew it was only upsetting me to think about it, but I couldn't get the images out of my head. I wondered if she was kissing him the way she kissed Jon. Why couldn't it be me? My sheets were damp with sweat by the time morning arrived, and I'd hardly slept at all.

I had thought that the one good thing about it all was that Celeste would be out of our home and I wouldn't have to look at her again, but then there she was, standing at the door first thing this morning, looking smug. Part of me, a very small part, longed to ask how he was, if he'd asked about me and what kissing him was like. The other part of me, the bigger part, wanted to push her outside and slam the door.

"MAY I JOIN you the next time you go to see Mother?" I ask Daddy at lunchtime.

He doesn't look up from his soup. "You're needed here."

I dip my bread into the broth and consider my options. As much as I don't want to accept Celeste's offer of help, it would solve this immediate dilemma. "Celeste has been given permission to help out here until Mother comes home. She'd come over while we're gone."

His head jerks up. "How do you know?"

"She came by this morning."

He regards me for a moment. "She's a Nielsson now. We can take care of ourselves."

"Just this once, Daddy?" I plead. "I really want to see Mother."

"Maybe I could look after the children while Nanette's away," Pam says very quietly.

Deborah drops her spoon with a clatter. "Oh no you don't, Pam!" she scolds. "Lena and I need you."

"If I had my own children," Pam says, still speaking quietly and not looking directly at anyone, "I wouldn't be able to help you. You'd manage. And this would just be for a few hours."

We all turn to hear what Daddy will say to this.

He's looking thoughtfully at Pam. "Thank you," he says. Then he turns to me. "Okay, Nanette. You can come with me."

Deborah abruptly pushes her chair away from the table and begins clearing dishes. I know that when Daddy returns to his office, there will be a scene in here. I glance at Pam. I mouth the words "thank you," realizing that her offer was a brave one. Deborah will now make her life miserable, just as she used to do to Celeste.

Pam just nods.

DADDY AND I don't speak much on our way to Springdale. I have only ever left Unity a few times, and I'm shocked as we drive through town. Where is the modesty of these people? I close my eyes and say a quiet prayer as we make our way across the town.

At the hospital, I have to run to keep up with Daddy's long, purposeful strides. He leads the way to Mother's room, but when we arrive, we find that her bed is empty. My heart beats a warning.

"Where is she?" Daddy demands of the first nurse we see.

"In surgery," she replies and quickly moves away.

"Surgery!" he hollers. He stomps down to the room where a group of nurses are gathered, typing at computers. I trail behind him.

"I demand to see my wife!" he says to the whole lot of them.

"That isn't possible," one of them says. She comes into the hall to face him. "But when the baby has been delivered, I'll take you down to the nursery to see it."

"I did not give my consent for surgery," he says, seething.

"You didn't need to," the nurse says. I notice a red flush creeping up her neck. "Your wife is legally able to give her own consent."

"Not in my faith she isn't," Daddy retorts. "She must have been coerced."

"It was *her* life that was in danger," the nurse says, barely able to maintain her control. "Not yours. And she chose to have a cesarean section before something serious happened. If you'd like to sit in the waiting area, I will let you know when she is out of surgery."

Daddy just stands there, staring down at her. The nurse holds her own. Eventually he wheels about and marches down to the waiting area.

An hour passes before the same nurse pokes her head into the room. "Sir, you have a healthy baby boy. And your wife is resting comfortably in the recovery room. She'll be back on this floor in a couple of hours. Would you like to meet your son?"

Daddy gets to his feet. "No. I'll be back tomorrow to collect both of them." He pushes past the nurse to get out of the room.

"But Daddy," I hear myself say. "I want to see the baby."

I don't know where I found the courage to say it, but there it is, hanging in the air between us.

He glares at me. I can feel the nurse looking from Daddy to me and back to Daddy again. "Then go see it," he says. "I'll meet you at the truck."

The nurse and I watch his retreating back. I can tell how angry he is just by the way he's walking. I wonder how he'd be walking if Mother hadn't made it. Like Colleen.

"Follow me," the nurse says.

We head in the opposite direction. When we reach the nursery, the nurse consults with a woman there, and she points to a bassinet.

"Wash your hands," the nurse instructs, "and then you can have a little cuddle."

I do as I'm told and then sink into a rocking chair with my little brother. He is incredibly tiny, his eyes are shut tight and he's wearing a little white cap. I pull him up to my face and inhale the freshness of him, and then I squeeze him tight and rock and rock, enjoying the heat that radiates from him. I pretend that he is my own and kiss his button nose. One arm pokes out of his blanket, and I stroke the tiny wrinkled fingers. They reach out and grip my finger. His strength is amazing. Eventually a nurse comes over, and I have to hand him back, but these few minutes with him have confirmed one thing. I want my own baby.

I THOUGHT DADDY might ask about his new son on the drive home, but his hands clenched the steering wheel, and he drove so fast I was frightened.

When we arrive, I go into the house, but Daddy strides off down the road. I find the whole family gathered around the table having supper.

"Well?" Deborah asks. "How is she?"

"She's had the baby. It's a boy."

There's a silence as everyone stares at me.

"Does that mean she's coming home?" my brother Blake asks.

"Daddy says he's going to pick them up tomorrow."

"That's great," Lena says. "Maybe life will go back to some kind of order around here."

"I don't know about that," I say, joining them at the table with the plate of food that had been left in the oven for me. "Mother consented to her own surgery, and Daddy is very, very angry."

I see the glances that Lena and Deborah exchange. If I didn't know better, I'd guess that they are happy my mother has been the one to make him angry.

TRUE TO HIS word, Daddy arrives home with Mother and my new brother, Liam, the next day. She is almost doubled over in pain as he won't allow her any medication. She hardly glances at anyone but struggles up the stairs to her bed. I carry Liam up and place him

in the bassinet that I've prepared for him, right beside
her bed.

Daddy stomps about the house, glaring at anyone who
gets in his way. In the kitchen, Deborah tells us about the
scene at the hospital.

"The doctor said she needed a few more days there," she
whispers, "so they could monitor her blood pressure and
check for infection, but Kelvin ordered a nurse to remove
her IV, and then he dragged Irene out of bed by her arm and
insisted she get dressed. She was crying and told him she
wasn't ready to go. A whole crowd of nurses gathered at the
door, and the doctor told Kelvin that if he cared about his
wife, he would leave her there. Kelvin said something about
teaching her obedience and asked a nurse to bring him the
baby. Eventually the doctor stormed out of the room, and
the nurses stood and watched while Kelvin half dragged,
half carried Irene down the hall. I carried the baby."

"That's what happens when you disobey your husband,"
Lena says with a sniff.

We each consider that for a moment. Part of me agrees,
but mostly I feel sad for my mother. She's lying in bed,
quietly crying in pain. I wish Daddy had just consented to
the surgery, and then everything would be better.

Chapter Twenty-One

CELESTE

I cringe when I hear my door creak open. Martin was with me last night. Shouldn't he be with another wife tonight? Sighing, I fill my head with thoughts of Jon, the way his eyes light up when he smiles, the curls at the nape of his neck, the squeeze of his hand holding mine. I remember the glances we gave each other as I walked the small children past his father's farm. I remember the tears shimmering in his eyes when I told him I wouldn't leave Unity.

None of this takes me completely away from Martin's groping, but it helps to ease the revulsion I feel as his body rubs against mine, his whiskers scratching my skin, the weight of his body pressing down on me. With a loud groan, he's done. After a moment, he kisses my forehead and slips out of the room.

This morning, Norah asks me to hang the laundry on the line as Sarah, who usually does it, is suffering from morning sickness. When I'm finished, I spend a couple of hours in the garden pulling weeds, so it isn't until the lunch dishes are done that I'm free to go see Rebecca.

As soon as I walk into the house, I sense the tension. Instead of loud argumentative voices, I hear people speaking in whispers. Rebecca, who has been watching out the window, charges into me as soon as I step into the house.

"Mother's home!" she whispers in my ear when I scoop her up.

"She is?"

She nods solemnly. "But she has a big owie, and we have to leave her alone."

"A big owie? Did she have the baby?"

She nods. "A boy. Liam."

"Oh."

"Can we go for a walk today?" she asks.

"We sure can," I tell her. "But I'm going to go upstairs and peek in on Mother first. Then we'll go."

"I'll come with you," she says.

"Not this time, Becca," I tell her. "You'll be able to visit with her soon."

Her eyes well up.

I put her down. "I won't be long. You get your shoes and hat on and meet me right here."

She sighs, wipes her eyes and nods.

I slip up the stairs, grateful that I haven't encountered anyone else. When I step into her room, I find Mother sitting on the side of the bed, her arms wrapped around her middle, hunched over. The baby is in a bassinet beside the bed.

"Mother! What is it?"

She looks up, her face full of anguish. "Oh, Celeste!" she says. "What are you doing here?"

"I came to see if I could help out. What's wrong?"

"I'm in such pain." She bends over again.

"Why?"

"Did no one tell you?"

"Tell me what?"

"That I had surgery yesterday, to remove the baby."

"Rebecca told me you were home with the baby, but I didn't know about the surgery."

She throws her head back. "Your father is very angry because he didn't give his consent for the surgery, but I had it anyway."

"Oh." I sigh. He's been angry a lot lately.

"He made me come home from the hospital early, without anything for the pain."

"He did?"

She nods and then flops over on her side, still holding her stomach. "It hurts so much."

I sit beside her and rub her back. A rage begins to build inside me. Why wouldn't he consent to the surgery if that's what she needed? And then to deny her pain medication? Who is this evil man? Not the father I used to cherish. Maybe I just never really knew him.

"Will you help me to the bathroom?" she asks.

With her arm draped over my shoulder, we make our way down the hallway. In the bathroom, she struggles to pull down her underwear, so I give her a hand, trying not to let my embarrassment show. She hands me her blood-soaked pad to fold up and put in the garbage. I pass her a clean one. Nanette should be doing this. She's better at this kind of thing. Mother hikes her dress up to sit on the toilet, and I look away, but not before I see the angry-looking wound that has been carved across her abdomen. Coarse black threads poke out through the folds in her belly.

Back in her room, the baby is fussing. "Can you try to console him?" she asks, hunched over again. I pick him up and jiggle him up and down, careful not to hold him too close. Babies always spit up on me. His fussing grows more insistent, so Mother sighs and begins unfastening the buttons on her dress. I pass him to her, relieved.

She winces when he latches onto her breast. "Cracked nipples," she tells me, noticing my frown. She leans back on her pillow and closes her eyes.

I feel nauseous watching her. I don't want to experience any of this.

There's a quiet tapping at the door. I turn and find Rebecca standing there. I'd forgotten all about her.

"I'm sorry, Becca," I tell her. "I was just helping Mother. I'm coming now."

Solemnly, she watches Mother from the doorway. She's used to babies and the time and attention they require.

"I'll be back as soon as I can, Mother," I tell her. She just nods, her teeth clenched and her eyes scrunched shut.

I'm poking my head into the kitchen to let someone know that Rebecca is with me when I hear the front door bang open. Rebecca's hand tenses up in mine. I whirl around and find Daddy standing behind me, my little brothers cowering behind him. "What are you doing here?" he asks gruffly.

"I came to help out."

"We can take care of ourselves. You're a Nielsson now. Go help out over there."

"I am still your daughter," I tell him quietly. "And Rebecca's my sister. I'd like to take her for a walk."

"I don't think you're a particularly good role model for my daughters," he says, grabbing Rebecca's arm and tugging her away from me.

Her eyes well up again. I glare back at my father. "I simply came to help," I tell him. "And if you want to talk about good influences…look at the way you are making Mother suffer." I glance at my brothers. "Are you being a good role model for them? Is that how you would have them treat their wives? I don't think you're one to be passing judgment on me."

Daddy raises his arm and slaps me across the face. The blow causes me to lose my balance, and I trip over Rebecca.

"Get out of here," he orders.

Rebecca lets out a loud wail. I squat down and wrap my arms around her before Daddy can pull her away. "Be good, honey," I whisper in her ear. "I love you."

She grabs onto my leg and clings. Daddy yanks her off me and pulls her into the kitchen. I slip out the door, aware of the stares of my wide-eyed brothers.

I STAGGER STRAIGHT to the beach. No one is expecting
me at Martin's, and I need time alone to think.

I walk straight to the inuksuk. Another one has been
added since Rebecca and I were here yesterday. How stupid
I've been, building useless statues from river rocks. I don't
know what got into me, why I was ever thrilled by the sight
of them. I kick the new inuksuk and watch as it topples to
the ground. Then I knock over a second one, and a third.
I crumple to the ground beside them.

I chose not to leave Unity with Jon because I didn't
want to anger my father or desert my mother and my little
sister, but here he is angry anyway, and there's nothing I can
do for Rebecca or Mother. I've made a terrible mistake.

"What's wrong, Celeste?" a voice asks. I swing around
and see the river-boy, as Taviana called him, standing a short
distance from me. My face burns with embarrassment, but
I have no desire to flee this time. This boy is as stupid as I
am, building statues that have no purpose.

I just shrug and continue contemplating the mess that
is my life.

"May I sit beside you?" he asks.

"I can't stop you," I tell him.

Out of the corner of my eye, I can see him remove his
shirt, and he places it on the beach and then sits on it. It
makes me notice how hard the rock is that I'm sitting on.

River-boy doesn't say anything, but his hands begin
building miniature inuksuks on the beach around where
he's sitting.

"How did you know my name?" I ask him.

"I met Taviana on the beach in Springdale. I asked about you."

"Oh."

We continue to sit in silence, me staring at the river, the boy balancing pebbles.

"My name's Craig," he says after a while.

I just nod.

Finally the rock I'm sitting on gets too hard, and I get up. My anger has passed, and I'm feeling stupid about knocking over the inuksuk. I begin to rebuild them. A moment later, Craig is beside me, helping. He doesn't say anything.

"I don't think I'm going to be playing this game anymore," I tell him.

"Okay." He continues working.

His answer surprises me. I thought he'd want to know why. I assumed that he was enjoying it as much as I was.

I can feel sweat trickling down my back, so I move into the shade of the trees and sit in the mossy area that I'd once shared with Jon. Was it only a week ago that he was here with me? My longing for him has reached a new level. The empty ache is overwhelming. I have to grit my teeth to keep from moaning out loud.

Craig is squatting on the beach, holding a large rock over a smaller one. I watch the steadiness of his hands and how he holds his back so straight. He appears to be in a state of total concentration.

My thoughts return to the first time I spotted him on the beach, building an inuksuk, and how the bare skin of his chest and back embarrassed me. How far I've come in such a short time. I'm a married woman now. A man's naked body is no longer a mystery to me, and it doesn't seem like something to avert my eyes from either.

Craig's hands leave the rock he's been balancing. It stays in place, precariously perched on the one below it. He wanders around looking for a new stone. Then he squats beside another rock, and he becomes completely still again as he attempts to create another balance.

I wander back to the beach and stand near him. He takes his hands away but the stone tumbles down.

"Oh, too bad!" I say, truly disappointed. I didn't realize I'd been holding my breath.

He looks up and grins. "They're just rocks. No biggie." He picks it up and tries again, slowly disappearing inside himself, his entire focus on the rock in his hands. I watch as he slowly moves the tip of the rock around the surface of the one beneath it. Sometimes his grip loosens, but then it tightens again. Over and over the loosening and tightening continues, and the rock is moved ever so slightly. Eventually I see him place the rock in a new place, and immediately I know he's found the balance. His grip loosens, and then his hands move away.

"You did it!" I say.

He smiles up at me.

"I thought it was impossible," I tell him.

"Nothing is impossible, Celeste." He stands up and stretches his back.

"Why do you do this?" I ask, although something inside me already knows.

He shrugs. "It brings me peace."

Peace. I gaze into his eyes, which are pools of calm.

"Can you teach me to do it?"

"There's really nothing to teach, Celeste. You simply need patience. Then you feel for the hidden gravity of the stone. It's there. You'll discover it as long as you are patient enough."

"I don't know..."

"Try it. One of the cool side effects is that it brings you into balance too. You'll feel connected to the earth while you're balancing, with a sense of well-being."

"All from balancing rocks?" He's got to be kidding.

I expect to hear him laugh, but he just nods, seriously. I hear a beeping noise, and he pulls a metal object out of his pocket and looks at it. "I have to go," he says. "I hope to see you here again someday, Celeste." Without another word, he walks upstream and melts into the trees that line the banks of the river.

I find a large stone and scan the beach until I find a foundation rock that pleases me. I squat in front of it, just as Craig did. I hold the stone over the base rock and try to balance it. It feels impossible. The top of the stone is so much heavier than the tip that I can't imagine it ever resting here. I glance over at the balance that Craig just made and see that his looks equally impossible. I take a deep breath, exhale and begin the long process of finding the hidden gravity. Over and over I touch the stone to the one below it. Over and over I can feel that it is not balanced. The sun is hot on my back, and my legs are cramping, but I keep on moving the stone, letting it rest for just a moment, testing the balance. I forget about the sun. I forget about the cramps in my legs. I can feel that I am getting close to a balance.

And then it happens. Even before I release my hands, I know I have found it. I gently release, and the stone stays in place. It's like magic. I stare at my creation. It looks impossible. But I did it.

Chapter Twenty-Two

Taviana

Jon has been depressed ever since he saw Celeste at the
hospital. Abigail and the boys have tried everything to
cheer him up, but all he wants to do is sit in front of the TV
and flick through the stations. I guess it helps take his mind
off the vision of his father marrying his girlfriend.

I'm not feeling too cheery myself. Abigail has reminded
me that I need to find somewhere else to live, immediately.
So, in a pathetic attempt to cheer both of us up, I've decided
we're going to have a beach day. I'll deal with my homeless
situation tomorrow.

We stop in at the library first so Jon can pick up his
card. "How many books can I borrow?" he asks the librarian,
turning the card over in his hand.

"As many as you want," she tells him.

His eyes light up for the first time in days, and he
disappears between the racks of books.

"Have many people applied for the job?" I ask.

"A few," she says. "But you have as good a shot at it as any of them, Taviana."

I nod, trying to look optimistic, but I guess I'm not too convincing.

"What's wrong?" she asks gently.

I hesitate, wondering how much to tell her. "The house rule where I'm living is that we have to be enrolled in school to remain there. I can't go back to school, so now I have to find somewhere else to live."

She tilts her head, frowning. "Why can't you go to school?"

"I just can't."

"Do you need help with your courses? There are tutors…"

"No. School is easy enough for me. It's the other kids…"

"Oh." She nods, understanding. "I know, schools can be hard places…"

I suddenly regret sharing this with her. My confession might hinder my chances of getting the library job.

"Do you have a computer?" she asks.

I shake my head. "Why?"

"You can take courses online if you have access to the Internet."

"Oh." I think about that. "Could I use the library computers to take my courses?"

She sits up straight. "I don't see why not. I'll look into it for you on my lunch break."

"Really? Thank you!"

Jon has returned to the desk, staggering under a huge stack of books. "How are you going to carry all those home?" I ask him.

"A couple of bags," he says. "I'm a big strong boy." He puts the books on the desk and flexes his arm muscle.

I put on my most impressed face. "Whooee!"

The librarian checks them out. "I'll call you at home later," she tells me. "When I get the information on the online courses for you."

"Actually," I tell her, "we're going to hang out down at the beach today. I'll just stop in before we head home."

"Perfect."

Jon chooses one book to take to the beach. He leaves the rest behind the desk to collect when we return. We walk through town and across the park, looking for a good place to plunk ourselves for the afternoon. I'm reminded of the first time I was here and how I met Craig and Hunter. Perhaps Craig will be making his art on the beach again today. "C'mon," I tell Jon. "I have something to show you."

We head upstream, and although Craig's not there, his art is. Jon is as impressed as I thought he'd be, wandering around each rock balance and studying it thoughtfully. I've stripped down to my bathing suit, and when Jon turns back to say something to me, his eyes widen and his face turns a deep shade of crimson. He quickly looks away.

"Get over it, Jon. This is what girls wear to the beach."

I take the two towels out of my bag. "Want to stretch out on the flat rock in the river?" I ask him.

He doesn't look at me. "I think I'll sit in the shade and read."

"Suit yourself." I hand him his towel and wade out into the river. I stretch out on the rock and let the sun do its thing.

The afternoon passes. I dip into the water every few minutes to keep cool. Jon never leaves his place in the shade of the trees, his nose tucked in his book on Inuit culture. His curious mind has been denied stimulation for so long that he'll probably overdose on books for a while. I'm sure Celeste would too, given the opportunity. It's interesting that these two found each other, two kids who, despite their upbringing, were misfits in their own community.

My mind wanders, and I consider my situation at Abigail's. I wonder if she'll consider me enrolled in school if I'm doing the work online. I smile to myself. If this works, my problem of where to live will be resolved. Thank goodness I didn't spend too much time agonizing over it. There's nothing like procrastination.

When I've finally had enough sun, I wade back to the beach and pull my clothes on over my bathing suit. Jon looks up and joins me on the beach again. "Ready to go?" I ask.

"Let's just build an inuksuk first," he suggests.

I shake my head at him but drop my bag and begin looking for rocks that will make good legs. He's going to have to get over her eventually.

THE LIBRARIAN GRINS when we push open the library door. "Can I do it?" I ask.

"You sure can," she says. "And I found and downloaded all the information you'll need." She passes me an envelope filled with paper.

"Thank you!"

"There's just one small drawback," she says with a frown.

"What's that?"

"The courses aren't exactly cheap."

"Oh."

"Is that going to be a problem?" she asks.

"Maybe."

"Well, read over the information. Hopefully you can make it work."

"Hopefully. And now it looks like I'll really need that job here."

She smiles at me and holds up her hands, showing me that her fingers on both hands are crossed.

ABIGAIL LOOKS UP from the stack of paper she's wading through. We're all gathered around the kitchen table, waiting for her verdict. "Well," she says, "apparently you really can graduate with online courses."

"Then you'd consider that enrolled in school?" I ask her.

She leans back in her chair. "Yes, I would," she says. "But Taviana, I simply can't afford these rates."

"Then I'll just have to work," I tell her. "I'll get two jobs if I have to."

"And if I get a summer job," Jon says, "I'll contribute to her courses too. That is, once I've paid my room and board here."

I high-five Jon. No wonder Celeste fell so hard for this guy.

Everyone starts talking at once. Jimmy and the boys all have ideas about how I can raise money to pay for the classes. As I look around the table at their faces, I realize how much they care and how badly they want me to stay. I swallow and discover a lump in my throat. I realize, too, how desperately I want to stay, and not just because it keeps me off the street. In just a week these people have become family.

Maybe Craig was right. Anything is possible.

Abigail turns to me. "Well, Taviana, it sounds like everyone's eager to help you out. And I admit it's nice to have another female in the house."

The room erupts with excited chatter. There is back-smacking and high fives all around. Abigail holds up her arm for attention. We all turn to her. "This calls for a celebration," she says. "You boys haul out the old barbecue and clean it, and Taviana and I will go into town and buy the ingredients for a feast. How does that sound?"

Chairs are pushed back, and the boys stampede into the backyard. I turn to Abigail. "Thank you," I say.

She simply nods, but I notice her eyes are bright with tears.

Chapter Twenty-Three

CELESTE

Martin continues to visit me every night. I'd like to ask one of my sister wives about this, about a rotation, but I don't feel I know any of them well enough yet. Aside from Gail, who still avoids me, everyone has been kind, so I guess they don't mind, but I sure wish it was someone else's turn. I lie there patiently until it is over, refusing to engage in conversation or even cuddling.

I don't dare return to my parents' home, but I asked Norah if she'd visit my mother and tell me how she was. She returned, looking sad, and said that my mother is healing but appears very unhappy. Apparently Daddy is still terribly angry with her. I lie awake at night, after Martin leaves, worrying. How long before he forgives her? My brothers and sisters will all be suffering.

I also toss and turn at night, tormented by my decision to stay here, and yet, even now, I cannot contemplate running away, though all the reasons I chose to stay are now meaningless. Knowing that I could never come back is just too scary. I've been cut off from seeing my family. I have been sentenced to a life without hope. My heart feels as though it will never heal.

No one pays any attention to me at the Nielsson home, so every afternoon I slip down to the river and balance rocks. Craig was right. Rock balancing does make me feel better, at least for the time that I'm trying to find the rock's point of gravity. When I concentrate on the rocks, I forget everything else, and for those short hours I experience peace.

"Hello, Celeste."

I look up to find Craig watching me. It's been a couple of weeks since I last saw him. "Hi."

He looks around the beach. "I see you've found the secret to balancing rocks."

I feel my skin burn. "I guess I have."

"No more inuksuk?"

I just shrug. He smiles. "Did you know that the inuksuk was once used as a directional marker?"

"It was?"

"Yep. The inuksuk would point in a certain direction to help travelers find their way, or to mark a place where there was good hunting or fishing."

"Is that why you build them?" I find myself stacking pebbles in front of me, just as he did the last time we met. This balancing thing is addictive.

He laughs. "No, I just like using things in nature to create art."

"But don't you worry about people—people like me—coming along and knocking them over?"

"Nothing in life is permanent, Celeste," he says, smiling. "Besides, the fun is in the building."

I think about that. "That's not quite true. For me, marriage is permanent. I'll be married for all of this life and all eternity too." I sigh.

"You're already married?"

I nod. His eyes widen, but he doesn't comment.

Craig wanders about, looking for a rock that pleases him. Finding one, he squats and attempts to balance it on another sharp-pointed one. I find my own rock and go back to concentrating. I put eternal life and marriage right out of my head. We carry on creating our rock art for the remainder of the afternoon. Finally I sit back and admire our creations. There are a couple of dozen rock balances strewn across the beach. Craig sits beside me. For this one moment, the world feels right. In balance.

"May I ask you a personal question?" he says.

Something shifts. Craig has broken an unwritten rule. We don't talk about personal things. The world is no longer in balance. "You can ask," I tell him, "but I might not answer."

He nods. "If you're not happy about being married, why did you agree to it?"

I stand up and brush off my skirt. "It's the way of our faith. To refuse the husband you're assigned to is to disobey God." I reach into my apron pocket, and my hand hits something hard and jagged. I pull it out. It's the arrowhead that Jon found the first time we met here. It makes me smile.

"What have you got there?" Craig asks, standing beside me.

"An arrowhead."

"Cool! Where did you get it?"

"Right here." I pass it to Craig, remembering Jon's words. *So you question your faith, but you're not prepared to do anything about it.* I realize now that Jon did do something about it. I didn't.

Craig turns the arrowhead over and over in his hands. "I don't understand that kind of faith," he says. "One that makes you unhappy." He passes the arrowhead back to me, and we make eye contact.

I slide the arrowhead back into my apron and try to think of a way to change the subject. I remember the strange object Craig had in his pocket the last time I saw him.

"What is that thing you carry in your pocket?" I ask him. "The thing that makes a noise?"

"My cell phone," he says, pulling it out. He hands it to me.

I hold it away from me, afraid of what it might do.

He laughs and takes it back. "It doesn't bite," he says. "Look." He flips open the top, and I can see tiny keys and some kind of screen. "It's also a clock," he says. "I can set the alarm to go off. Sometimes my dad tells me what time to meet him, and sometimes he just calls."

"Taviana told me about cell phones, but I've never seen one."

"Now you have," he says, smiling kindly.

The cell phone suddenly starts playing a tune. I jump away.

"That will be my Dad," he says. He puts the phone to his ear and listens. "I'll be there in ten minutes." He closes it and puts it back into his pocket. "I've gotta run," he says. "The bus is leaving."

"The bus?"

"Just an expression." He looks at me. "Will I see you here again soon?" he asks.

I nod. "I hope so."

We gaze at each other for another moment, and then he turns and disappears down the river.

TWO MONTHS HAVE passed since I became a Nielsson. Today my mother arrives for a visit. She has Liam with her.

I pour us each a glass of lemonade and join her at the kitchen table, where she sits nursing the baby. My sister wives have discreetly taken their children and moved to other parts of the rambling house.

"How are you doing, Celeste?" Mother asks.

"I'm okay. What about you? Last time I saw you…"

"Was when I was in the hospital."

"No, I came and saw you the day you came home."

"You did?"

I nod.

"I don't remember." She looks puzzled. "Those first

couple of weeks home are just a blur." She frowns, thinking about it.

"I would have come back again, but Daddy ordered me to leave."

She nods. "I know. And I haven't been to church services since Liam was born. I'm waiting to hear what the Prophet has to say about my disobedience."

We sit in silence for a moment. There is so much I want to talk to her about, but I can't find a point of entry into any of the topics.

"Is Martin treating you well?" she whispers.

I nod.

She smiles. "I knew he would."

"Is Daddy treating you well?" I ask her.

The question startles her. She puts Liam to her shoulder and burps him. "He's still angry."

"What is wrong with him, Mother?"

"Nothing is wrong with him, Celeste," she answers crossly. "I was wrong to disobey him, but I was frightened."

"No, Mother," I respond, just as crossly. "He was wrong to deny you the medical attention you needed."

"Your father has perfect faith. He has more trust in God than in medicine and doctors. I crossed the line by agreeing to the surgery."

I don't answer. I think Daddy just likes to throw his weight around, but I decide it's best not to say anything.

Liam is sleeping in Mother's lap. She clears her throat, and I see she's blushing. "How are your…your husband-wife relations?" she asks.

It takes me a moment to figure out what she's referring to, but when I do, my cheeks grow hot too. I shrug. "Shouldn't Martin be spending equal time with each of his wives?" I ask.

She stares at me, trying to puzzle out my question. "It's entirely up to him, but of course you have to tell him when it's your time of month."

I nod, and then her words register. My time of month.

I haven't had it since I got married.

The realization slowly sinks in. I feel the blood drain from my face.

"What is it, Celeste?" she asks.

I can only stare at her. Liam begins to squirm, and she offers him her other breast.

"Celeste?" she asks again.

I run to the bathroom and throw up.

I HAVEN'T BEEN out of bed for a week except to use the bathroom. Norah brings me food and tells me that the sickness will pass soon enough. I don't tell her that there is no nausea, only despair. And fear. I clutch the arrowhead like a drowning person would clutch a life preserver.

Eventually I can't stand my self-imposed confinement any longer. I get up and wander down to the river, just to get out of the house. I find Craig there, building an inuksuk. I sit on a large rock and watch him. Eventually he joins me, sitting on his own rock. Neither of us says anything for a few minutes, but the silence is comfortable.

"Do you practice a religion?" I ask him, as if no time had passed since our last conversation on the beach.

"Not formally," he tells me. "Though I identify with some of the nature-based ones that have an earth-centered spirituality."

I just stare at him. I have no idea what he's talking about. "Who are you anyway?" I ask.

He throws his head back and laughs. "Just me. Directionless Craig."

"Directionless?"

He shrugs. "I haven't decided what to do with my life. Too many decisions. It makes me crazy. So here I am, balancing rocks."

"Does that make you sad?"

He tilts his head. "Not sad, no. Just a little frustrated sometimes. My parents are on my case."

"On your case?"

"They're pressuring me to make a decision."

I think about that. "In The Movement, we don't have to make decisions. We accept the ones that have already been made for us. We submit to a higher power. Our life is easier in that way."

I can feel Craig studying me. "You say that with such enthusiasm."

"Huh?"

He smiles at me. "I'm sorry, I was being sarcastic, but if your life is so much easier, why do you seem so unhappy?"

I have to look away. "I'm different for some reason, but

my sister, Nanette, she's happy." I think about that. "Well, she was, anyway, until…until just lately. But in general, I think people are happy here because they know exactly what they have to do to get to the Kingdom of Heaven."

"You don't sound so sure."

"I told you, I'm different. Something's wrong with me."

"I think something's right with you."

"You do?"

He nods. "I think there are some things more important than just being happy."

"Like what?"

He reaches for a rock and begins a new balance. "Like being free to think for yourself."

MY DOOR CREAKS open. Martin hasn't been to visit me since the day my mother was here and word got out that I was pregnant.

"Celeste?"

"Yes?"

"May I speak with you?"

I turn on the lamp by my bedside.

He comes in and sits on the end of my bed. He reaches over and picks up my hand with both of his. "I heard the good news," he says.

I nod and resist the temptation to roll my eyes.

"It happened so quickly," he says. "We are truly blessed."

I just nod again and focus on a stain on the wall behind him.

"You know, don't you, that this means I can no longer lie with you."

"I know." I hope my relief doesn't show on my face.

"But we can still cuddle or go for walks together. There is nothing wrong with that. I want us to become closer."

I have to admire this man, my husband, for his perseverance. Anyone else would have given up on me.

"Are you happy here, Celeste?"

"Everyone is very kind." I nod. "You have a lovely home."

"We have a lovely home, Celeste. And I want you to know how delighted I am that you are already carrying our first child. This will be just the first of many, many children for us."

I try to smile, but suddenly I really am feeling nauseous.

"Let me know if you need anything. And I can be available for you most evenings. Sarah is also expecting a child, so I am truly a fortunate man."

He stands up, prepared to leave. "Have you heard anything from Jon?" he asks.

I shake my head.

"His mother, Gail, and I miss him terribly. I hope he knows that."

"I'm sure he does."

"Take good care of yourself, Celeste. And of our child. If you need anything, let me know." He drops my hand

and I lean over to turn off the lamp. This is the only good thing about being pregnant. Martin won't be lying with me again until the baby is weaned. That alone deserves a special prayer of thanks.

THE SUMMER DAYS blend into one another. I still don't have many responsibilities at Martin's, so I spend every afternoon at the river, keeping cool. I stay out of the sun as much as I can, but I do enjoy sitting in the shade, watching Craig create his art. I wonder why he keeps coming back to Unity, but I don't ask.

One day he brings me a book. "I think you might like it."

I turn it over in my hands and read the description on the back. I'm quite sure this book would be forbidden in Unity, but my boredom is acute and my curiosity has always been a problem for me. I begin to read. When I look up again, I see that the sun has moved halfway across the sky. Craig is standing in front of me. "Enjoying it?" he asks.

I don't know how to answer him. I feel like I've been transported from my own world into an altogether different one for the afternoon. The ideas in the book shock me but fascinate me at the same time. "Could I borrow this for a few days?" I ask.

"Won't you get in trouble for reading it?"

"I'll hide it in my room. No one pays much attention to me."

He nods. "I'll bring some others too, if you like."

I feel something happening inside me, something I haven't felt for weeks. I try to identify it and realize that I'm simply feeling lighter. The thought of reading books, even if they are forbidden, excites me.

"By the way," Craig says, "I have a message for you from Taviana."

"You do?" My heart stutters.

He nods. "I met her building inuksuk on the beach in Springdale with her friend Jon."

I can only stare at him.

"Her friend, Jon, he's quite obsessed with them. Even more than me."

Numbness washes over me.

"Anyway, Taviana wants me to tell you that she and Jon are both enrolled in school for the fall, and that she has a job working at the library. She gets to tell stories to little kids as well as shelve books. She wants you to know that she's doing really well."

"Oh." I'm still thinking of Jon, obsessed with building inuksuk.

"Celeste? Are you okay?"

I look at him but barely see him. I can only see Jon, on the beach, stacking rocks.

"Do you have a message for Taviana?"

I think about that. I could tell her that I'm pregnant. And that my father shuns me. And that I'm still heartsick for Jon. "No." I shake my head. "Just say hi."

"Okay." Craig nods, studying me. "Are you sure you're going to be okay?"

I do my best to smile. "Yeah. I'm just a little hot. Thank you for the book. Will I see you tomorrow?"

He smiles back. "I hope so. My dad thinks I come to the river to ponder my life. That's why he's willing to drop me off near Unity."

I slide the book into my apron pocket with the arrowhead and walk home.

WHEN CRAIG'S DAD gets fed up with dropping him off near Unity, Craig begins to hitch rides up the road. For some reason he seems to enjoy being with me, just like I enjoy being with him. He begins bringing me books that he's read, and I take them home and secretly devour them late at night. We spend our afternoons discussing the ideas in them.

"So if a person doesn't believe in God," I ask him, "what makes them behave?"

He considers that. "Their conscience. Do you only behave when you think someone is judging you?"

"God *is* always judging me," I tell him, though I have to admit, I haven't always behaved.

"But just for the sake of argument, Celeste, imagine that He isn't. Would you start doing unkind or bad things?"

"I don't know." The concept is just too strange for me. God has always been part of my life.

"Celeste, I don't believe you would. You're a good, kind loving person, whether God is watching you or not."

Our conversations bounce back and forth. I'm especially interested in the lack of religion in the books. The characters don't have God in their lives, and they are consumed with impure thoughts. Craig and I laugh a lot, and sometimes I argue points that I don't really believe just for the sake of argument. I've tried to convince Craig that I haven't changed my mind about anything since reading the books, but truthfully, I know the books and the conversations with Craig are altering the way I think. When I sit in church on Sunday mornings, I often find myself questioning the things that the Prophet tells us, even more than before. I continue to read late into the night and then lie awake, thinking of questions for Craig. Our conversations give me a reason to get out of bed each morning.

THE LEAVES ARE changing color and the air is noticeably cooler. Craig rarely builds anything anymore. My stomach is beginning to bulge, but if Craig has noticed, he hasn't said anything. We just sit under the trees and discuss the books.

Today we haven't even talked but just sit quietly, reading.

"Celeste," Craig says, closing his book and turning to me. He's smiling and his eyes are shining. "I am so grateful to you."

"For what?"

"For helping me find my direction."

"Your direction? How did I do that?"

"All these discussions we've had about the books and religion, they've really got me thinking…and I want to learn more. I've decided to go back to school to study theology."

"Theology?"

"It's the study of religion."

"Oh." I'm happy for him, but the "going back to school" part makes my stomach flip.

"I applied to a few colleges, and one has accepted me even though it's so late in the summer."

"That's good!" I try to sound enthusiastic, but I don't like where this conversation is going. "Your parents must be happy."

"I'll say."

"When do you start?"

"In a couple of weeks." His expression changes. The light leaves his dark eyes.

"What's wrong?"

"The college I'm going to is in Seattle."

"Oh." I look down at my book, trying to hide my shock.

"But I'll be back next summer," he says, trying to be positive.

I nod. "I'll have a baby by then." I guess he'd figured it out because he smiles, sadly.

"I'm really going to miss you," I tell him.

"I'm really going to miss you too," he says.

I gaze out at the beach that we've completely transformed this summer. We've built a whole community of inuksuk, all shapes and sizes. I take comfort in the fact that when I come back to the beach in the fall, I won't be completely alone.

"I don't think it was me that helped you find your direction," I tell him.

"No?"

I shake my head. "No. It was the inuksuk."

WHEN I ARRIVE at the beach on Craig's last day before he leaves the valley to go to school, I find him building an inuksuk in the clearing under the trees where I first sat with Jon, and where Craig and I have been having our discussions. It's by far the tallest inuksuk on the beach. On each of the outstretched arms there is a small rock balanced. I laugh when I see it.

"What are you doing?" I ask him.

"This is my farewell gift to you," he says. "And something to help you remember me."

"As if I could forget you!" I tell him.

"We're going to have a little pagan ceremony too," he tells me.

"We are?" I was ready to read and talk about pagan ceremonies, but I'm not so sure about participating in one.

Craig balances small candles on various points of the inuksuk's body. He strikes a match and lights them. Then he motions for me to step closer. He takes one of my hands and then rests his other hand on the arm of the inuksuk. He nods at the inuksuk's other hand, indicating that I should do the same.

I do and then smile at Craig, feeling silly. He smiles back. "Are you ready?" he asks.

"I guess so."

"Okay, then." He clears his throat. "We have created a circle," he says, his voice full of authority, "that includes Celeste, myself and this inuksuk. It's a circle rich in symbolism."

The words sound rehearsed.

"First," he continues, "this circle represents our strong bond of friendship. It was the inuksuk that brought us together, and we give thanks to it for that gift."

He pauses, and I find myself silently thanking the inuksuk for Craig. Then I wonder if that makes me a pagan.

"Secondly," he says, "the inuksuk represents strength, and this strength will keep our friendship strong until we meet again." He squeezes my hand. I squeeze his back.

"Thirdly," Craig says, "the inuksuk represents respect, and I built this one to show my respect to our friendship." He smiles down on me, and I find I have to blink back tears.

"Finally, this inuksuk represents the ancient inukuk, the one that pointed people in the right direction, and I give thanks to it, and to Celeste, for helping me find my own direction.

"The balanced rocks that sit on the inuksuk," he continues, "represent the balance we strive to find in our lives. Life is fragile, just like the balanced rocks, but they help us remember that anything is possible."

Craig squeezes my hand again and smiles at me. I smile back.

"Is that it?" I ask quietly.

He nods but doesn't let go of my hand. We stand quietly for a moment, thinking about the inuksuk. I also think about all the new ideas Craig has offered me, and I give a silent prayer of thanks for that.

Finally Craig steps back and lets go of my hand. My first pagan ceremony wasn't nearly as scary as I thought it would be.

"I think you'll be a great pagan preacher some day," I tell him.

He tilts his head back and laughs a belly laugh so contagious that it gets me started too. We laugh and laugh, wiping tears off our cheeks.

JON IS GONE. Taviana is gone. Craig is now gone too. The fall days grow colder, and I visit the beach less and less often. I help out around the Nielsson house as much as I can, but I have very little energy, and as my belly grows, I feel more and more awkward.

Winter settles in and I find myself spending more time alone in my room, reading and rereading the books Craig left me. Mother is allowed to attend church services again, so the highlight of my week is when I can visit with her during the social hour. Rebecca has attached herself to Pam and won't have anything to do with me. Pam is now expecting her first child too. I notice that Martin still spends a lot of time at Nanette's juice table. She doesn't talk to me, but she smiles sweetly at him.

By January I have trouble dragging myself out of bed in the morning. I feel so heavy, and there isn't anything to get up for. Nothing matters. Nobody notices me. I was better off at home, where I had chores to do to pass the time. Occasionally Martin comes by my room to check in, but he doesn't stay long. I have an overwhelming sense of hopelessness, and I sleep for many hours every day. The winter drags on. I constantly think about Jon and how I missed my opportunity to join him. Now I am expecting a child that will be his half-sister or half-brother. I wonder, too, about Taviana and Craig. I hope Taviana has managed to behave herself. And Craig. How I miss our conversations.

The baby does somersaults inside me. It has hiccups. It elbows me. I remember how Mother said I was like a miracle to her when I was born. She called me precious. Nobody else was allowed to care for me.

I feel a strong kick. Unlike Mother, I feel no connection to my baby. I'd be happy to give it away.

ON THE FIRST day of spring, she is born.

Norah cuts the umbilical cord, hands her to me and the world turns upside down. Suddenly everything matters again. Gazing down at her wrinkled little face, I know that there is nothing more important in this world than the tiny child in my arms. Something has burst into bloom inside me, and I feel an enormous rush of love. Her eyes blink open and she gazes back at me, and in that instant I want her to have everything I never had. I want her to have an education and a career and to fall in love and choose her own husband if she wants to. I want her to be independent and to travel. I want her to be free to think for herself.

I may not have been strong enough to leave Unity for myself, but in this moment I know that I will find the strength to do it for her.

MY DAYS ARE now filled with taking care of my daughter. Before she was born, I worried that I would be a terrible mother, a mother who had no patience and who gagged at the smell of dirty diapers. I worried for nothing. What I couldn't do for other people's babies, I can easily do for my own. I love bathing her and feeding her, and I spend hours just watching her sleep. I also spend hours dreaming about our escape.

When the weather begins to grow warmer, I put her in a baby sling and walk to the river. Most of our rock balances did not survive the winter weather, but the inuksuk did. I like to stand under the trees with the tall one Craig built on his last day and remember the little ceremony he created. It always makes me smile.

Then one day I arrive at the beach and see Craig balancing rocks. I'm so happy I just about burst. Now my dreams of escape can become a reality.

"Craig!" I holler across the rocky beach.

He looks up, drops the rock he was balancing and jogs across the beach. "Celeste! It is so good to see you!" He reaches for both of my hands.

We smile at each other. Peacefulness washes through me.

"And who is this?" he asks, looking down at the baby swaddled on my chest.

"This," I tell him, "is Hope."

EPILOGUE

I stand on the beach in Springdale and watch Hope, who's wearing denim shorts and a bright red T-shirt, place a round stone onto the top of our inuksuk. It's the head. She turns and smiles up at me. "Beautiful," I tell her.

Hope turned five a few months ago and will be starting kindergarten in the fall.

I, too, will be going to school in the fall, continuing my studies through correspondence. Abigail finally bought a computer, and I want to complete my high school diploma by the time Hope starts grade one. I'll be sharing the computer with Taviana, who is doing university courses. She's studying to become a librarian. My plan is to graduate from university before Hope enters high school. It's a struggle balancing work, caring for Hope and studying, but with a little help from my friends, I know I can do it.

I see a woman in a long dress coming toward us on the beach. It has to be someone from Unity. A little knot of worry forms in my stomach. Even though Martin reluctantly allowed me to keep Hope after I left Unity, I still worry that someone will come and take her away from me.

I study the woman as she approaches and see that she's young and she's carrying a baby on her hip.

"Hello, Celeste," she says.

I am so shocked when I recognize her that I'm literally speechless.

"Taviana told me I'd find you here." She looks down at Hope, who is stepping closer to me. "I'm your Aunt Nanette," she tells her. "And this is your half-sister, Clare."

"Her half-sister?" I say, finally finding my voice. "You married Martin?"

"I did." She grins proudly. "Turns out God hadn't turned His back on me after all."

I pull Nanette into my arms and squeeze her and her daughter to me. "I've missed you!" I tell her when I let them go.

"I missed you too, and," she says, looking sheepish, "I know now that I was foolish to be so angry. For a long time I've wanted to apologize."

I look into the face of her baby and I'm startled. "Clare looks exactly like Hope did at that age."

She studies Hope. "I guess she would. Same father, their mothers are sisters…"

"How did you get permission to come here?" I ask her.

"Martin's doing the shopping today," she says. "He knew how badly I wanted to see you, so he let me come with him.

I found Taviana at the library, and she told me where you'd likely be."

"He wasn't afraid I'd tempt you to leave him?"

"No." She laughs. "He knows how much I love him. I would never leave!" She lowers her voice. "And he wanted me to say hello and find out how Hope is."

I nod. I'm grateful to Martin for letting us go as easily as he did. "Tell him Hope is great, and hello from me."

"I will."

"Why isn't Daddy shopping?" I ask, suddenly worried.

"He suffered a stroke a while ago."

"Oh no!"

"He's going to be okay. But he's taking it easy."

"How's Mother?"

"She's fine. Liam was her last baby, so she's had time to get her strength back. They're all in school now, so Mother isn't quite as busy as she used to be."

"And Rebecca?" The familiar ache returns as it always does when I think about my family.

"I think Rebecca takes after you. She asks too many questions for her own good." She smiles. "What about you? Did you get back together with Jon?"

I shake my head. "No." I remember the awkwardness between us when I first arrived at Abigail's with Hope. "We live in the same house, but I think it was too weird for him with Hope being his half-sister and me having been married to his father. We're good friends. More like brother and sister, and he's a really good big brother to Hope."

She nods, though I can see that she doesn't understand at all.

I consider telling her about Craig and how our relationship has blossomed over the years, but then I decide not to bother. "Can I ask you a question, Nanette?"

She tilts her head, waiting.

"Are you happy?"

"I am very happy."

She looks surprised that I asked, and I can see from the glow in her eyes that she really is happy.

"What about you?" she asks.

I think about it. It is hard being a single and very young mom. Taviana, Hunter, Abigail and the other guys all help out when they can, but the weight of the responsibility is mine. So no, I'm not always happy. Sometimes I'm stressed and worried, and I miss Craig terribly when he is away. I inhale. But do I regret my decision to leave Unity? I look down at Hope, who is back to balancing rocks on the beach. No. Not at all. I'm finally free to think for myself.

"I'm good," I tell her. "Very good."

AFTERWORD

Although Unity is a fictional community, there are people in numerous towns throughout North America who have beliefs similar to the ones described in this story. Polygamy has been illegal in Canada and the United States since 1890, but the fine line between the law and the right to religious freedom has allowed polygamy to flourish.

SHELLEY HRDLITSCHKA is the best-selling author of *Dancing Naked* and, most recently, *Gotcha!* Shelley lives in North Vancouver, British Columbia.